MATCH OF THE MONTH

MOUNTAIN MEN

· OF MUSTANG ·
MOUNTAIN

December
IS FOR
DEAN
KACI ROSE

DECEMBER IS FOR DEAN

MOUNTAIN MEN OF MUSTANG MOUNTAIN

KACI ROSE

CONTENTS

Publisher's Note: This is a work of fiction. Names,
characters, places, and incidents are a product of the
author's imagination. Locales and public names are
sometimes used for atmospheric purposes. Any
resemblance to actual people, living or dead, or to
businesses, companies, events, institutions, or locales is
completely coincidental.

Book Cover By: Kelly Lambert-Greer

Editing By: Debbe @ **On The Page, Author and PA
Services**

To the Match of the Month supporters, especially...
Jackie Ziegler
Thank you so much for your support. We couldn't do what we love without you!

CHAPTER 1
DEAN

"CONGRATS, Dean. Looks like you're next on Ruby's list," Jenna says as I walk into the Merc to grab an order for the women's shelter.

"Are you kidding me?" I stop in the middle of the sidewalk, and that's when I notice the Mountain Man of the Month flyer in the window of the mercantile. "Dammit," I mutter.

I know there is no point in making a scene. What's done is done. I've watched it happen to my brothers-in-arms for the last eleven months. With eleven wins under her belt, Ruby sure as hell won't stop now.

"I'm sorry," Jenna says, placing a hand on my arm before passing me and heading to her car.

Taking a deep breath, I step into the mercantile, and go to the back to get the order for the women's shelter so I can take it and the Christmas trees there. It's a favor Jensen and Courtney asked of me, but now I wonder if they were conspiring with Ruby.

"Dean! Good to see you. Have you seen the new peppermint line? I just got it in for Christmas, and it's already been a big hit. I brought back the peppermint bark you liked last year," Ruby says with a wink. "Orville, go grab the bags that Jensen and Courtney ordered," she says to her husband, who's working with her today.

As the town mayor, Orville wears many hats, including offering extra help when Ruby needs it. All these years later, that man is still in love with her, as much or more so as the day they met. That's the kind of love I'm holding out for. But I don't dare tell Ruby because she will take it as a personal challenge, and that's the last thing I need right now.

"You could have at least given me a heads-up about this match of the month crap, Ruby," I say as we wait for Orville to grab the stuff from the back.

"Now, why would I do that? With all the holiday events coming up, why would I give you a reminder so you can get out of it like you tried to do for the harvest festival? Not a chance, boy," she says with an evil glint in her eyes.

I can't even say anything because she's right. If I had known, I probably would have found a way to get out of town for the entire month. Now, it's too late, and she knows it.

"Fine. When that doesn't work, and I'm your first failure, you can end all of this and leave the rest of the guys alone."

"Oh, but I'm not going to fail. I can feel it in my bones. You're going to be the best match yet." She

2

walks off to help another customer, and my gut says she already has plans to set something in motion.

Orville helps me move some boxes and some mail into my truck, along with a few bags of stuff Courtney has ordered for the shelter before I head out of town.

After Jensen and Courtney got together, they needed some help at the shelter, so Jensen asked me. I agreed and have been a semi-regular there. Mostly fixing things that break, that sort of thing.

But I guess something is going on that they need to talk to me about. Also, they asked me to pick up their order in town and bring some Christmas trees for the families to set up and decorate.

Right now I'm driving through the mountains, circling a few times, ensuring I'm not being followed or watched before I pull up to the gate and enter my code.

You can't see the building itself from the road, so it's a bit of a drive after I get through the gate, and then there's another gate around the building as an extra layer of security. When anyone comes to the first gate, they're notified. By the time I get to the building, Courtney and Jensen are waiting for me by the back door.

"We just got done pulling out all the Christmas decorations and ornaments. The kids are really excited to get going on the trees," Courtney says with a smile. Though I can tell it's strained, like something's wrong that she does not want to talk about.

Since getting to know her, I've learned that she will talk when she is ready. But not always in front of the people at the shelter.

"Everything okay?" I ask, even though I'm pretty sure it's not.

"We can talk about it later. Let's get these trees in," Courtney says. We unload everything and set up the trees so the families can start decorating.

A boy who looks about Izzy's age walks over, holding the hand of a younger girl who is the spitting image of him.

"My sister wants to help put decorations on the tree. Can we?" he asks with so much hope in his eyes that it's obvious it means a lot to him.

"Of course you can, Max. Why don't you help Jensen here with the lights? Gracie, can you start going through that box of ornaments to get an idea of where you want to hang them once the lights are on?" Courtney says before she gets pulled away.

The lights go on pretty quickly as the little girl sits on the floor looking through the box. When we're done, she pulls out the star that goes on top of the tree.

4

"Oh, can I put the star on the top? Please, please, please, please, please?" she asks and even sticks out her bottom lip for good measure.

"You okay with that?" I ask her brother.

"Yeah, it'll mean more for her to do it," he says, shrugging his shoulders and digging into the box.

"Can I pick you up to help you put the star on the top?" I ask her.

A huge smile lights up her face as she nods enthusiastically.

Picking her up around her waist, I lift her so that she can place the tree topper. Then she takes an extra minute to ensure it's on straight before I set her back down.

I take a step back and let her and her brother start decorating the tree as Courtney walks up beside me.

"I don't know what to do with that family. The kids are super sweet, but the mom has extended family involved with some not-too-good people," Courtney says, never taking her eyes off the two kids.

"Who's her family involved with?" I ask, now that she's got my attention.

"Savage Bones," she looks at me with worry in her eyes.

She has every right to be concerned. Savage Bones is a one-percent motorcycle club that has been causing problems in the area. To say they are not good people is an understatement. If the MC thinks one of their own is getting out, they would rather see the person dead. It would only take one person sharing that information to cause trouble.

"After the first of the year, I can get her and the kids into a shelter in Bozeman. Until then, they need a safe house. We're hearing motorcycles going by several times a day, and at this point, it's just too close for comfort."

"Shit. Is it getting that bad? Why hasn't Jensen said anything to the rest of the club?"

"I think he will be telling them soon, as we are out of options. We've tried a few other shelters, but we just got a call today from the last one. They're all booked up because of the holidays. There's no place else we can send her. I'm sure as hell not going to turn her out on the street, but it's not safe for her to stay here either."

"She can stay at my family's old hunting cabin. My brother Six is the only person who knows where it's other than my parents."

I don't know what came over me to offer the cabin. Until the words were coming out of my mouth, I didn't even realize what I had said. Before I offer the use of it, I should really check with my older brother. But since Six is the Mustang Mountain

Riders club secretary, I know he'll be more than willing to help.

"Really?" Courtney says with so much hope in her voice that all I can do is nod my head.

"Holly, come here," Courtney calls, and the most beautiful curvy woman with dark brown wavy hair steps up. "Dean, this is Holly. She's Max and Gracie's mom. Holly, Dean here just offered you his hunting cabin. Not only is it off the grid, but only his family knows how to get there."

"I really appreciate it, but I just talked to a friend who is going to let me stay with her. It's going to be a day or two before I can get there. We're working out the details now." She smiles and walks off when her daughter calls her over.

I don't understand the sudden loss I feel of her not coming to stay with me or this fierce need to know all about this friend she is supposedly staying with. While I've never been overly protective of someone like this, I know that I'm not going to be able to just let her walk away.

"Ugh, oh, I know that look," Courtney says.

"What look?" Jensen asks, walking up beside her.

"The look on Dean's face is the same one each of you guys had right before the fall. Looks like Ruby might be going twelve for twelve."

7

CHAPTER 2
HOLLY

I CAN'T KEEP PUTTING the shelter at risk by staying here. That is the last thing I want to do to the people who have been so kind to help me get back on my feet.

But I'm going to need a few days to get things lined up with my friend and get us out of here. There is no way staying with Dean is a good idea, not with the way he has me feeling just standing next to him. Something like that can't be normal.

Stepping outside, I let the icy December mountain air hit my face, and I take a deep breath. It's a breath of freedom and one that reminds me not to rush. I am in control.

That is, until the roar of a motorcycle rushing past on the main road fills the air and fills me with terror icier than the wind. Even though I can't see the main road from here with all the trees, bushes, and the main gate, there is no mistaking that sound.

That sound reminds me my time here is limited. When I go back inside, the warm heat is like a comforting hug. Feeling an urgency to talk to Janet, I call her again.

Janet answers on the phone on the third ring. "Holly, honey, are you okay?"

I let out a deep breath. "Yes, I'm fine, but I need your help. I have to get out of here soon."

"What's going on?" Janet asks, concern in her voice.

"The motorcycles are passing by way too often. It's not long before they find this place and me. I can't have people here hurt because of me."

"I'd love to have you here, but I don't think you will be safe here either. A guy on a motorcycle has been parked a few houses down, watching us since last night. They are taking shifts like they know this is where you are coming," Janet says, worriedly.

As I process Janet's words, a cold shiver runs down my spine. It's like my worst fears are coming true. "Oh no, they are getting closer," I whisper, my voice barely audible. "What do I do now? Where can I even go?"

Janet doesn't respond immediately, and it's as if I can hear her thinking on the other end of the phone. "I have a friend who lives up north, in Canada," she finally says. "She has a cabin in the woods, far away from civilization. It's not the ideal place, but it's safe."

So, my two choices both end with a cabin secluded in the woods. Woods, I have no idea how to survive in. But I have no other choice. I have to leave the shelter and go somewhere safe until I figure out what to do next. If I take Dean up on his offer, I'll have help and be close to Courtney if I need anything.

If something were to happen to one of my kids, I can't imagine being up in Canada without anyone to help me.

"Okay, I will let you know. The woman that runs this place has given me another lead," I tell her, being as vague as possible in case anyone is listening in. I wouldn't put it past Savage Bones to illegally wiretap anyone.

Janet pauses for a moment, considering my words. "Alright, but be careful. My friend's cabin is an option in case you need it."

"Thank you, Janet," I say, gratitude filling me. "I really appreciate it."

"Of course, Holly. Stay safe and keep in touch."

As I hang up the phone, my mind races with what I need to do next. I go in search of Courtney and find her in her office.

"Hey, can I talk to you for a moment?" I ask her, closing the door behind me.

"Of course. What's up?" she says with a bright smile that always seems comforting, no matter what is going on in your life.

"There are some Savage Bones guys stalking my friend's place. It's no longer a safe option for me," I tell her, and her face falls. "I hate to say Dean's offer might be my best chance, but I don't know anything about him!"

Courtney bites her lip, lost in thought for a moment. "I hate to say it, but I think you're right. At least with Dean, he is someone who can protect you."

I nod in agreement, knowing she's right.

"Dean and my husband have been friends for years, and Dean has been a part of Mustang Mountain Riders for almost as long. He's a good guy with an older brother he's close to. He's great around kids, and you know we wouldn't let him anywhere near here if we didn't trust him with our lives," she says.

Taking a deep breath, I feel a sense of relief wash over me at Courtney's reassurance. "Okay, I'll do it," I say, nodding resolutely. "I'll take Dean up on his offer. But we need to move fast. I don't think I can stay here much longer."

Courtney nods in understanding, her face serious. "We will need to move you out of here without you being seen in case one of the Savage Bones guys happens to be driving by. Let me make the arrangements. You pack and prep your kids." She reaches for her phone to get the ball rolling.

With that, I leave Courtney's office and head back to my room, my heart pounding as I pack.

I can't believe this is happening. How did I even get myself into this mess? Trying to focus on the task at hand, I grab my bag and start filling it with clothes, toiletries, and anything else I might need. We don't have much, but I want to take everything we can.

My mind is racing, trying to think of everything I might need for this unexpected journey. Thinking on how to make this transition as smooth as possible, I make sure to pack extra clothes for my kids and their favorite toys.

As I finish packing, I hear a knock on my door. My heart races as I quickly check to make sure everything is packed before checking through the peephole. It's Courtney and her husband, Jensen.

"Since we brought the SUV today, we will smuggle you and the kids out in the back with some blankets and pillows. Often, we're bringing things home to wash or throw away. You guys will be under the pile. Dean and some of our other friends will meet us at his place," Jensen says.

"You will then get into Dean's truck and lie down in the back seat, covered with some blankets and such, until you get off the main road. Our friends will drive with you as protection and to keep a buffer between you and anyone else on the road. They will make sure you aren't followed and block any traffic from going up the mountain. Though, just to be safe, even they won't know where the cabin is," Courtney says.

"Hiding under blankets? What about the kid's car seats?" I ask.

"We can put them in the back of Dean's truck, so you have them, but it's too risky to have the kids visible in case someone spots them. I know it's not the safest way to get there, but it has the fewest risks," Jensen adds.

"Okay, the bags are ready. Let me go talk to the kids," I say.

"I will load these in the car." Jensen takes my bags.

Finding my kids playing with a few others, I call them over. "Max, Gracie, I need to talk to you for a minute."

THEY COME RUNNING, and I lead them back to our now almost empty room.

"Listen, guys, we have to leave here for a little while because it's not safe for us to stay here anymore," I tell them, trying to keep my voice calm but firm.

"Why? What's happening?" Gracie asks, her wide blue eyes filled with concern and confusion.

"Well, Nana's husband is mixed up with some bad guys. So we need to stay away from him." I explain to her about my stepdad as simply as I can.

"It's going to be fun. We're going on a little adventure," I say with a smile, trying to keep my

13

voice calm even though my heart is racing. "Just for a little while, we're going to go stay with a friend of mine. It's going to be a secret, so we need to be really quiet and really brave. Can you do that for me?"

Max and Gracie both nod eagerly, already excited for the adventure.

"Will there be animals?" Gracie asks excitedly, her eyes full of wonder.

"Maybe. We'll have to see when we get there," I say with a smile. "We are going to have to ride in a car under some blankets, like we are playing hide and seek."

"Like hide and seek from the bad guys?" Max asks. He's older, and I think he understands more than I wish he did.

"Yes. So, I need you both to be brave, okay?"

They nod again, and I pull them into a tight hug. "I'm proud of you both. Let's go meet some new friends and have an adventure," I say, trying to keep my voice steady as I lead them out of the room and towards the waiting car.

"Jensen and Courtney are going to be in the area with us. We can talk unless they tell us not to, but we can't move around, okay?" I say as we step out into the cold Montana air.

Again, both kids agree, and I take a deep breath as we get into the back of the SUV and pull the blankets over us. I can feel my heart pounding in my chest. This is it. We are really doing this.

Climbing in, I press my back to one of the SUV walls. Gracie climbs in next and crawls right into my arms. Max lies down beside her, and then the pillows and blankets get piled on top.

"Okay, looks like a big pile of laundry," Courtney says, and Gracie giggles.

I try to hold back a laugh, but the relief of my children's laughter is too much to bear. While I stroke Gracie's hair, I'm hoping she won't feel the fear that I'm fighting to push down.

Jensen starts the car, and we move out of the parking lot. It feels like hours, but it is less than twenty minutes before we reach Jensen and Courtney's home, and we pull into the garage.

"Okay, we are here. Does anyone need any bathroom breaks before you start the next leg of your journey?" Courtney asks.

"We should all go just to be sure," I say, as we head inside.

Once everyone has an empty bladder, we go out to Dean's truck.

"Your bags and car seats are in the back. It's covered so no one will see them," Dean says, drawing my attention to him.

"Thank you for this," I tell him, and he smiles.

"Let's get moving. It's best to make it out of here while we still have daylight," Dean says.

The back of Dean's seat is up, and there is a thin mattress, which will make lying on it more comfortable. There are blankets against the middle where the seats connect. With Gracie in my arms, I settle in, and Max gets in, lying with his head at my feet.

Before we know it, we are once again covered in blankets and on the road.

"There are six other guys with us. Two ahead of us, two behind us, and one way behind, making sure no one is following. Another is waiting by the road leading up the mountain, watching who comes and goes. So far, no one has been on that road all day," Dean says.

When the sound of a motorcycle gets louder, Dean says, "Okay, stay calm and don't move, guys."

I hold my breath as the motorcycle passes us by. As she clings to me tightly, I can feel Gracie's small body trembling in my arms. Max's eyes are closed, and he's making an effort to try to remain calm. Hoping to offer some comfort, I run my fingers soothingly through his hair.

As the motorcycle disappears into the distance, I let out a sigh of relief. "Thanks, Dean. You really thought of everything," I say to him with admiration.

He chuckles. "We've done this before. We know how to keep you and your family safe," he replies.

"You work with the shelter doing things like this?" I ask.

I find the sound of his voice soothing and want him to keep talking.

"Yeah, me and my buddies help as often as we can."

Before long, the road turns from smooth asphalt to a bumpy, unkept road, and Dean slows down.

"We are off-road now. It's only going to get bumpier. I will do my best to make it comfortable for you guys," he says.

Even though he is taking the road slowly, it seems to stretch out forever as the truck jostles beneath us. Finally, the truck comes to a stop.

"Stay here, and let me check the cabin before you come out of there," Dean says.

I nod, feeling a knot form in my stomach. We had been preparing for this moment, but that didn't make it any less nerve-wracking.

Dean jumps out of the truck and disappears into the woods, leaving us in silence. I squeeze Gracie a little tighter, and Max stirs beside me, his eyes opening sleepily.

"What's happening?" he whispers, his voice thick with exhaustion.

"We're almost there," I say, trying to sound confident. "We just have to wait here for a while longer."

Max nods, his eyes drooping shut once more. I stroke his hair again, trying not to think about what might be ahead of us. Though I can feel the adrenaline pumping through my veins as I wait for Dean's signal to move.

18

CHAPTER 3

DEAN

"EVERYTHING LOOKS GOOD. Let's get you guys into the cabin and settled," I say, removing blankets from them.

"Look at all this snow! Can we make a snowman? Pretty please?" Gracie asks.

"No, it's perfect for a snowball fight!" Max says, already leaning down and forming a snowball in his hands.

"You better not throw that snowball, mister!" Holly says, giving a stern mom look that makes Max drop the snow.

"We can do both, but first, we need to get in, get settled, and get the heat going. I promise we will have plenty of time to come back out here. Can you guys help carry some of the blankets? These are all clean and for us to use while we're here." I hand some of the blankets and pillows to each of the kids.

Then I help Holly with the bags.

"Let's get you inside, and I'll come back out for the rest of it," I say, referring to the bags of groceries Courtney stuffed in my front seat. It's not much, but it'll get us through the next few days before my brother can come up and bring us more food.

We're about halfway to the door when little Gracie comes running out of the house.

"Oh no. Oh no. Oh no!" she says in the sweetest little voice.

"What's wrong?" I ask, instantly on guard.

"There's no Christmas tree!" she says like it's the biggest problem in the world.

"Well, that's because we only have live Christmas trees up here, so we have to go find one, cut it down, and bring it back."

"Wow, we've never had a real Christmas tree before!" Gracie says, running back into the house.

"I know you're stressed, but there's plenty for them to do that will keep them busy and keep their mind off of why we're here," I tell Holly as we walk into the cabin.

This cabin is so remote that only my parents, my brother, and I know it's here. Not even my MC brothers know where it is. Just a few of them even know the cabin exists.

"Where is the thermostat? I'll turn the heat on," Holly says, looking around the house.

"No thermostat, just the old wood stove and the fireplace. If you go ahead and finish unloading the stuff from the truck, I will get both of them going. Max, can you help me?" I ask him. His eyes go wide with excitement. "We got this, Mom!"

Max walks with a newfound confidence, even though I'm pretty sure he has no idea what we're doing.

"We need to go get some of the wood from the shed out back, so let's go see how much we have."

He follows me out to the shed, which not only stores wood and food, but other tools from different repairs we've done over the years. When we hunt, we use the shed to store game meat.

"There's not as much wood as I hoped, but this should be enough to get us through two or three days. Would you be willing to help me gather some more tomorrow? That way, we can stock up on wood before the next snowstorm hits."

"Yes! Are you going to teach me how to use an ax?" he asks, all excited.

"I can show you, absolutely, but you're going to have to be a bit taller to properly use one," I say. Then I stack up some wood in his arms before loading up my arms and heading back into the cabin.

"This is the last of what's in the truck," Holly says, setting bags on the counter. "I'll put these groceries away. Gracie, you want to help me?" she asks.

"No, I want to watch him do the fireplace," she says, running over and holding onto Max's arm.

21

Once I'm finished getting the fire going, Holly joins us.

"Alright, all the groceries are put away. What can I do next?" She looks around the cabin.

"The tote that was in the back of my truck has clean sheets and towels. If you want to strip the beds of the sheets that are there, there's a washer and dryer in the hallway. We can wash them, so we have an extra set on hand. While they're washing, let's make up the beds we will use. There are three bedrooms, and the only bathroom is the one in the hallway," I tell her, pointing to the hallway that's beside the big stone fireplace.

When I get the woodstove going, I turn to Max and Gracie.

"Alright, now we need to clean things up. I'm going to give you both a towel, and I want you to dust anything that you can: tables, chairs, windowsills, books, anything that has dust on it, okay?"

Thankfully, they actually seem excited about cleaning.

I hand them both a small towel and spray it with some dusting spray, and off they go. Pulling out the dishes from the cabinet, which I know we'll use tonight, I hand wash them and set them on the drying rack. Fortunately, Courtney put a pan of lasagna in my truck, so we don't have to do anything but warm it up. Later, I'll pull out a pan to cook the garlic bread she included as well.

"Sheets and towels all done," Holly says, walking down the hall towards me.

For a minute, I'm struck by how absolutely gorgeous she is. When Holly smiles at me, I feel my heart skip a beat. She's so lovely, with her bright blue eyes and long brown hair. I'm drawn to her like she's my true North. And those curves of hers? I really want to get my hands on them.

Distracting myself from my straying thoughts, I say, "So, we need to do some cleaning, but we can do it later. Since Courtney sent us dinner and we don't have to cook, there is enough daylight left for us to go find a Christmas tree. Y'all up for it?"

Before I get the words out of my mouth, Gracie is jumping up and down.

Holly chuckles. "I guess that's a yes from Gracie. And I wouldn't mind going out for a little bit. Let's do it."

"Okay, there are a few rules. It can't be too big because it has to fit in the living room corner over there." I point to the wall opposite the fireplace. "It also can't be any bigger than me if we want to put a topper on it," I say, lifting my hand above my head, showing I can touch the ceiling in the cabin.

This cabin has been in the family for generations, and people were much shorter back then, so the ceilings weren't really made for my 6-foot 4-inch build. My dad got rid of the low-hanging lights when I hit my teenage years, so I didn't keep hitting my head on them whenever I walked around the cabin.

We bundle up in our warmest jackets and boots and head out to the woods. When we step outside into the crisp winter air, we all take deep breaths, enjoying the scent of pine and the wood smoke that fills the air. Right then, I feel a sense of peace settle over me. Gracie skips ahead with Max, her boots crunching in the snow, and I watch her go with a smile on my face.

Thankfully, some decent pine trees are just inside the forest tree line behind the cabin. Gracie and Max race around us, looking at trees.

"Dean! Come stand next to this one!" Max says, and Gracie walks up to see which one he is looking at.

"Oh, it's so pretty!" she says.

I walk over to stand next to it. The top of the tree comes up to my eyes.

Max and Gracie start jumping up and down again. "This is the tree!" they cry in unison.

AS I WORK on cutting down the tree, I can feel Holly watching me. It's as if her eyes are burning into my back. When I take a moment to catch my breath, nothing can stop me from turning around to meet her gaze.

For a moment, we lock eyes, making my heart race. I can feel the tension between us, and I know that I'm not the only one experiencing it. Holly bites her lip, and there's desire sparking in her eyes. Even though I know that I should look away, I can't. I'm drawn to her like a moth to a flame.

She looks away first and clears her throat before talking to the kids. I quickly snap out of my trance and finish cutting down the tree. We wrap it up nicely and tightly, and I carry it back to the house.

"Okay, we will set it up today and then decorate it tomorrow once I am able to pull out the Christmas decorations. But to do that, we have to clean up the house," I say.

Max and Gracie's excitement dampens a little, but they eagerly help.

We spend the next hour or so cleaning and organizing the cabin, creating a cozy and welcoming atmosphere. Max and Gracie's excitement is contagious, and even Holly seems to be enjoying herself.

More than once, I look up. Watching them makes my heart ache because I want a family like this more than anything. This is what it was like growing up with my parents and brother, and what I want for myself.

As the afternoon wears on, the sun starts to dip below the horizon, and the temperature drops even further. I add more wood to the fireplace to keep it toasty and warm.

"I'm going to start on dinner. Why don't you give the kids a bath now? The water heater is small, so if you want to shower with hot water tonight, it's going to need time to reheat," I tell her.

"But we don't want to go to bed yet!" Max says.

"No bed yet, just a bath. We do things differently out here. After dinner, we can watch a movie," I say, winking at Holly. I'm really hoping he will fall asleep during the movie. It's been a long day for all of them.

I watch as Holly nods in agreement and takes Max and Gracie to the bathroom. As she disappears down the hall, I'm surprised by the pang of longing I feel. I'd love to be part of all these family moments, but this isn't my family, and they aren't mine, no matter how much I wish they were.

When I hear the water running, thoughts of taking a bath with Holly fill my head. What would it be like to feel her skin beneath my fingertips and run my hands through her hair? But I know that's not something that can happen. I'm here to protect her, not seduce her.

Shaking my head, I turn my attention back to making dinner. I break out the food Courtney sent us with and get to work. As I cook, I can hear the sound of Holly and the kids playing in the bathroom, and once again I'm shocked by the twinge of envy I'm experiencing. They sound so happy, so carefree, and I long to be a part of it.

As I finish up dinner, Holly and the kids come out of the bathroom, wrapped up in warm PJs. The kids' hair is damp and curly, and they look so adorable that I can't help but smile.

"Dinner's ready," I say, gesturing to the table. The kids jump up and down excitedly, and Holly takes a seat.

We enjoy our meal together, chatting and laughing about our day. And as the evening wears on, we curl up on the cozy couch together and watch a movie. We don't even get twenty minutes in before the kids are passed out.

Holly leans her head on my shoulder, and I feel her warmth radiating right through my body. I put my arm around her, pulling her in closer to me. We sit in comfortable silence, enjoying each other's company and the warmth of the fire.

Halfway through the movie, Holly lets out a yawn.

"Let me help you get the kids to bed before you pass out on me, too," I joke quietly.

Picking up Gracie, I notice how peaceful she looks. Her small body is wrapped up in her blanket, and she's holding her teddy bear close to her chest. Max is fast asleep on the other side of Holly.

I get up, carry Gracie to her room, and tuck her into bed. As I stand by the door, I want this with all my heart. I want a family to come home to, to enjoy moments like these.

On the other side of the room, Max stumbles into his bed, and I take a few minutes to tuck him in and say good night.

When I go back to the living room, I find Holly tidying up the scattered popcorn and blankets.

"Thanks for helping with the kids," Holly says, smiling at me gratefully.

"No problem. They're great kids," I reply, returning her smile.

We finish cleaning up, and I walk Holly to her room. She turns to face me, her eyes meeting mine.

"Thanks for everything tonight, Dean. It's been a long time since I've had a night like this," she says, her voice soft and vulnerable.

Reaching out, I gently tuck a strand of hair behind her ear, letting my fingers linger on the soft skin of her cheek.

"It was my pleasure, Holly. I'm glad you and the kids enjoyed it," I reply, my heart pounding in my chest.

She looks up at me, her eyes shining in the dim light of the hallway. For a moment, we just stand there, gazing at each other, the tension between us palpable. I know I need to leave before I do something stupid.

"Well, I should go. Goodnight, Holly," I step back and turn to leave.

"Goodnight, Dean," she replies softly, her voice barely above a whisper.

Needing to put some distance between us, I hurry back to my room.

CHAPTER 4

HOLLY

ONCE I FINALLY FELL ASLEEP, I slept pretty well. The problem was getting to sleep. It seemed like before I knew it, I was dealing with the kids running in to wake me up because the sun was up and the fires had died down, so the cabin was cooling off.

Max and Gracie jumped into bed with me, putting their cold feet on my legs to warm up. We lay there and snuggled for a little while longer until the smell of breakfast filled the air.

Thankfully, when we came out to the kitchen, there was already coffee made as Dean was finishing up scrambled eggs, bacon, and toast.

After breakfast, I was helping with the dishes when Dean turned to me.

"Why don't you go get ready? My brother will be here soon with food and other things that we need for our stay. I'll take the kids outside to run off some energy," he says.

I hesitate for only a minute before nodding. The idea of an uninterrupted shower to wake up sounds amazing.

Gathering my items, I quickly get in the shower, letting the hot water soothe all my tense muscles. The air is filled with a sweet smell of lavender and eucalyptus from the soap. The steam of the shower fills the air with the fresh scent, causing me to inhale deeply. Right away, that wonderful smell infiltrates my body, making me relax.

As I towel off and get dressed, I can't help but think about Dean's brother coming over. I keep waiting for Dean to ask me why I'm in danger and what I know. Maybe he's waiting for his brother. I really expected it after the kids were in bed for the night, but he didn't even bring it up.

Suddenly, I hear the sound of a truck pulling up and Dean's voice outside. I finish getting dressed and walk to the door. When I open it, I see a tall, muscular man standing in the yard talking to Dean while Max and Gracie run around in the snow.

"You must be Holly. I'm Six, Dean's brother," the man says, walking over to shake my hand.

"Dean says you had a late breakfast, but I brought pizza for lunch. We can get everything unloaded and set up the cabin, then warm it up if that's okay," he says.

"That sounds great." I smile at him.

Max and Gracie help bring in the bag of food, Christmas items, and even some toys. As we all work to unload the truck and set up the cabin, there are a lot of smiles, and I'm glad the kids don't know for certain why we are here. It makes me happy to see them carefree and relaxed.

After lunch, both kids let out a big yawn.

"I guess all that running around and now with full bellies, you two need a nap," I say. There's a certain a conversation they don't need to be part of that I'm sure is going to happen.

"Mom!" Max says.

"Listen, I saw some brownies in the groceries. If you want any for dessert, you will take a nap." I use my stern mom's voice.

They both grumble but go to their room. As I tuck in Max and Gracie, a sense of unease settles over me once more. I know I need to talk to Dean and his brother about what's been going on, but I don't want to distress the kids or anyone else. Yet, I also know I can't keep putting this off.

After tucking in the kids, I make my way back to the living room, where Dean and Six are sitting on the couch. They look at me, and the easy-going expressions from earlier are long gone.

"It's time to talk about why we are here, isn't it?" I say, and they both nod. Sitting on the opposite end of the couch from Dean, I turn sideways so I can face both brothers.

"So why are the Savage Bones after you?" Six asks, and both sets of eyes are on me.

"My stepdad is a Savage Bones member. When my husband died of cancer, it left us with a lot of bills. Insurance covered a lot, but every time he had a doctor's appointment, a treatment, or medication, we had to make a co-pay, which came out to several thousand dollars a month." I pause and take a deep breath. They don't need my sob story.

"Anyway, once I settled his life insurance and the debt, we had nothing left. I had to sell the house to pay for his funeral, and my mom let me move in with her. My stepdad was always nice, and I knew he was in a motorcycle club, but I never gave it much thought. It wasn't until we moved in that I realized there was something off about the club."

"They're a one-percent club, meaning they think they're above the law and don't bother following it," Six says.

"When I saw his patch, I looked up what all it meant. So, I stayed out of his way, but I couldn't leave my kids alone with him either to go to work. My mom offered to watch them, but my stepdad had no set schedule. Everything was set, and I was looking forward to moving in with my friend Janet. When I was packing up, he came home early and was thrilled I was moving out. But then he got distracted by a phone call.

"After I finished packing, I was going to meet my mom at a park where she had taken Max and Gracie for the afternoon. I went back inside to say goodbye. Looking back, I should have just gotten in my car and left. But I walked in and knocked on his office door, which was wide open. He didn't hear me, so I knocked again. When he looked up, there was a rage in his eyes. He ended the phone call and started yelling about how 'I didn't hear anything,' and I hadn't heard anything but him say 'it's going to go down' and 'something Mustang Mountain,' which with him meant they were coming here to party or drink so I didn't think anything of it," I say, losing the battle of keeping back the tears.

Dean hands me a box of tissues, and I take a deep breath before continuing.

"Go on," Six says, gently giving me a nod. His eyes are soft and caring, making me feel safe opening up.

"He grabbed me and shoved me into his office, yelling over and over about how I didn't hear anything. I told him I didn't hear anything anyway, and I was just coming in to say goodbye. But he didn't believe me. He pulled out his gun and pointed it at my head. Then he told me that if I ever spoke a word about what I heard, he would kill me and my children. I knew he wasn't bluffing. He gripped my

34

arms so hard I felt bruises forming immediately. After I agreed not to say anything, he shoved me away, and I hit my lip on the corner of a cabinet, busting it open. Courtney has the photos from when she first saw me. They aren't pretty. I was terrified and didn't know what to do. That's when I ran, grabbed my kids, and drove out of town. I parked on the side of the road and Googled for a place to stay. I found out about the women's shelter and called the number. Courtney met me that night." By now, tears are streaming down my face.

Dean slides over next to me and pulls me into his arms. I can tell how mad his brother is, and I don't know if it's because of what I told him or because I got his family involved in all this.

"When I didn't answer my mom's calls, I guess they started looking for me. That's when they started watching Janet's place and driving by the women's shelter." I just melt into Dean, soaking up his comfort.

After a moment, Six clears his throat, breaking the silence. "We're going to take care of this. You don't have to worry about anything. We'll make sure you and your kids are safe."

Even though he reassures me, I can still feel the anger and tension simmering beneath the surface of his words.

I nod, believing him, though I don't see how they can.

"Right now, we have an advantage. They have no idea if she is with us or if we know anything. The window is short before they put it together or try to smoke her out. So, we need to move fast. I'll let the club know what she said, and we'll get eyes on Savage Bones to see what they're up to." Six says, standing.

"Wait, what club?" I ask.

Six looks at me like I should know what he's talking about.

"The Mustang Mountain Riders," he says, and pure panic sets in.

"No. You are a member?" I ask.

"We both are. So is Jensen. I thought you knew that," Dean says.

I get up and start pacing as my mind races.

"It was bad enough when they thought I knew something. If they think I ran to you guys and told you whatever it is, I know they will kill me and the kids, no questions asked," I ramble.

Dean stands, putting his hands on my shoulders to stop my pacing. "We won't let that happen. You are safe with us."

He says this so firmly that I feel a glimmer of hope." But how can you be sure? They killed the last person who crossed them," I say, fear seeping into my voice.

"We're prepared for anything. And we'll do whatever it takes to keep you and your kids safe," Six chimes in.

Looking at them both, I see the determination in their eyes. They are not messing around, and suddenly, I know they will do whatever it takes to protect us.

"Okay. What do we do now?" I ask, feeling grateful for their support.

"First, you stay here with Dean. No one but our parents and the two of us know where this cabin is. Only a few members of the Riders even know of this place. Second, we'll start gathering intel on the Savage Bones. We need to know everything about them, from their movements to their connections. And third, we will come up with a plan to eliminate the threat they pose to you and your family," Six answers, his voice serious and determined.

"Eliminate..." I say, hanging on that word, knowing what it means with the Savage Bones.

"Killing isn't our go to. We'd rather let authorities handle them," Dean reassures me.

The rest of the day is uneventful. The kids wake up wanting to play with their new toys, and I smile, hoping they can't tell my mind is elsewhere. But I keep worrying about what will happen when Savage Bones finds out I'm with the Mustang Mountain Riders. I'm anxious about what the Riders must do to protect me and how far they are willing to go before they tell me I'm on my own.

Just in case, I need to make escape plans for my kids and me. Because the only person I can one-hundred percent rely upon is myself.

CHAPTER 5

DEAN

HOLLY'S SCREAMS fill the air. I bolt out of bed, my heart racing, and have no idea what I am about to walk into. When I rush into the living room to Holly, I find her staring out the open back door, her face pale and ashen.

Stepping up behind her, I wrap my arms tightly around her waist, pulling her close to my chest. "Hey, hey, it's okay," I whisper soothingly in her ear as I stare at Hades lying on the back porch, staring right into the cabin at Holly.

"There is a wolf looking at me like I'm his next meal. How will this be okay?" she whispers out of the side of her mouth.

"Mom?" Max calls out, his voice still full of sleep.

"It's okay, buddy. Go back to your room," I say.

He nods from the doorway and goes back into his room.

"Holly, this is Hades. He's kind of like the town pet. My buddy Jackson found him as a pup and nursed him back to health. We've noticed that he keeps an eye on all of us now. Also, he just had some pups with my buddy Mack's sled dog, Persephone."

"So, he won't hurt me or the kids?"

"Nope, he's probably looking for some peanut butter, his favorite human food. Let me see what we've got." I head into the kitchen.

As I rummage through the pantry, trying to find a jar of peanut butter, I can feel Holly's eyes on me. I turn around to find her still standing in the same spot as before, frozen in fear.

Spotting some peanut butter granola bars, I take one, hand it to her, and unwrap the other one.

"Why don't you feed him the granola bar?" Walking over to Hades, I give him a good rub on his head, and feed him my bar.

Tentatively, Holly takes the granola bar and slowly steps out onto the porch. Hades raises his head, sniffs the air, and then pads over to her, tail wagging.

"See, he just wanted a snack," I say, standing behind her and watching as she feeds Hades the granola bar.

"He's beautiful," she says, running her hand over his fur. "I've never seen a wolf up close before."

"He's a good boy," I say, smiling as Hades nudges her hand for more food.

As she feeds him the last bit of granola, I can feel the tension draining from her body.

Holly looks up at me and smiles. I feel a warm flutter in my chest at the sight of her, and I smile back. It's these kinds of moments I cherish—when I can be there for her and make her feel safe.

After Hades finishes his granola bars, he runs off into the woods.

"See, he was just checking in and seeing what's going on. I'm convinced he's a bigger gossip than Ruby," I joke.

Holly smiles as we head inside, but it doesn't quite reach her eyes.

"What do you say we take the kids out and have a snow day after breakfast? I promised them snowmen and snowball fights."

"I think they'd like it," she says.

As we bundle up the kids and head outside, the winter air is biting cold. The snow is piled high, and everything is draped in white. It's beautiful, and I'm grateful to share it with Holly and the kids.

We spend the morning building a snowman and having a snowball fight. When Holly's laughter fills the air, it makes me feel alive and happy. Her joy is contagious, and I find myself smiling at everything she does.

I'm glad to be able to give them this to make their day just a little brighter.

Taking a break to sit down to rest, I notice that Holly's eyes keep going back to the spot in the woods where Hades disappeared earlier.

"Why don't we go inside and warm up with some lunch? I saw Gracie yawn, so I'm sure she could use a nap," I say, with Holly agreeing.

As we make our way back into the cabin, I enjoy the calm that washes over me. Being out in the snow with Holly and the kids is everything I've been dreaming of on a winter day with a family.

Inside, I start working on lunch while Holly helps the kids unbundle.

The kids eat lunch and talk about who won the snowball fight. When they're done, they don't even protest a nap. They are both tired from all the fun outside this morning.

Holly joins me on the couch once the kids are asleep.

"You seemed to enjoy yourself out there. I've been wanting to take the kids on a snow day all season, and you finally made it happen," she says, her eyes glittering in gratitude.

We sit in comfortable silence for a few moments before Holly speaks again. "So, you must have had many days like today out here growing up."

I nod, memories of my childhood flooding back. "Yeah, my brother and I used to spend all day outside, playing in the snow. My mom always made us hot cocoa, and we would warm up by the fire. It was the best. I loved summers out here, too, fishing and hiking. In the fall, we'd even pitch a tent in the yard just to sleep outside."

Holly smiles. "It sounds like a wonderful childhood."

"What about you? What was your childhood like? Where did you grow up?"

Holly's smile fades slightly as she looks off into the distance. I can see a hint of sadness in her eyes as she speaks.

"I grew up in the city—New York City, to be exact. My parents were always working, so I spent a lot of time with my grandmother in her apartment. She was the one who taught me how to bake and read me stories. She was my constant, my rock."

Before continuing, she takes a deep breath. "But after she passed away, things were never the same. My parents were still always working, and I was left alone a lot. We moved out to Denver with my mom's parents when I was in high school after my dad left Mom. I didn't have many friends and never felt like I fit in. I always felt like something was missing. That is until I met Ollie, the kids' dad."

"I'm sorry that you had to go through that," I say softly, placing a hand over hers.

She shakes her head like she is trying to shake away the memories.

"What about you? Did you always live in Mustang Mountain?"

"Yeah, my family has been here for generations. We've had this cabin for as long as I can remember. It's where I feel the most at home. After college, I did some traveling. My mind was set on seeing the country. I visited Chicago, LA, the Grand Canyon, and did some hiking in the Smoky Mountains. I think it's why I knew for sure this was home."

We sit and talk for a while more about growing up in the city versus a small town, our parents, and much more. Our talk is interrupted when Gracie appears.

"Mommy, can we have some hot chocolate?" Gracie asks in the sweetest voice that just pulls at my heartstrings.

I look over at Holly, and she nods her head with a smile.

"Let's do it. I'm going to teach you my momma's super-secret recipe. It's a Hershey Kiss hot chocolate, the best in the world. But you have to help me make it, okay?" I say, standing. She nods with a huge smile, and I swoop in and pick her up, carrying her to the kitchen while she giggles the whole way.

Setting her on the counter, I grab the bag of Hershey Kisses my brother brought just as Max comes out of the room from his nap.

"Hot chocolate time?" he asks.

"Yep, you've got to come in here and help, though. You're going to be in charge of stirring," I say, getting a pot out and the wooden spoon my mom always used for hot chocolate.

"But I want to stir," Gracie says with a little pout on her lip.

"Oh, I have an even more important job for you. You need to open the Hershey Kisses. You know, that was my job when I was a kid." I tell her, opening the bag and putting it on the counter next to her.

"How many do we need?" she asks, her eyes going wide.

"Well, do we want normal hot chocolate or extra chocolatey hot chocolate?" I ask, already knowing the answer.

"Extra chocolate!" Both Max and Gracie shout as Holly walks into the kitchen.

"What can I do to help?" Holly asks.

"Can you grab us coffee mugs and make sure they're washed and ready, please?" I ask her. "Okay, for extra chocolatey hot chocolate, we're going to need eight Hershey Kisses per cup, so since there are four of us, that means we're going to need eight times four people. So, my mom always counted out four piles of eight Hershey Kisses."

Max and Gracie hurry to make the piles.

"Now what?" Max asks.

"Now we each eat a Hershey kiss out of the bag for good luck," I say, and they all giggle as we reach in to get our chocolate.

As Gracie works on unwrapping them, we get the milk warming up, and then put in the Hershey kisses and stir until they are melted, adding a little of Hershey's cocoa powder.

Once done, I carefully pour the hot chocolate into each mug and top with a few marshmallows.

"Mmmmmm!" Gracie says as she kicks her little legs in excitement after taking the first sip.

"That's a lot of sugar in a cup of hot chocolate," Holly says, watching the kids enjoy the hot chocolate.

"It is, but Mom's secret was to always send us outside to run and play in the snow while we had the sugar high. Then we'd come in and she would feed us dinner. By that point, we were exhausted, so we would end up in bed early that night," I tell her.

"Your mom sounds like a really smart woman," she says with a gentle smile.

"She is, and I think you two are going to get along really well."

After hot chocolate, we take the kids outside and let them run off all their energy. For dinner we have spaghetti, and as predicted, there are lots of yawns at the dinner table.

The kids get ready for bed and are passed out on the living room couch before we even get ten minutes into a movie.

While helping Holly get them to bed, I notice how clear the night sky is. So, I reach into the closet and pull out the large electric blanket my mom keeps there.

"Why don't we head outside to the porch? It's a really clear night, and let's see what we can find," I say to Holly when she comes out of the kids' room.

We make our way to the porch and wrap ourselves in the heated blanket. The night air is crisp and cold, and I can feel the chill on my cheeks. Holly snuggles closer to me, and I wrap my arm around her, pulling her close. We gaze up at the night sky, and it's like nothing I've ever seen before. The stars are so bright and clear, and they seem to be so close I could reach out and touch them.

I point up towards the sky and begin to name the constellations as we see them. Holly listens intently as I explain the stories behind each name, at least the names my dad told me.

"I've never seen the stars so clearly before," Holly says, her voice filled with wonder.

"Yeah, Mustang Mountain is pretty remote, so there's not a lot of light pollution. That's what makes the stars so visible," I explain.

We fall into a comfortable silence, wrapped up in each other's arms as we continue to stargaze. I feel Holly's hand slip into mine, and I interlace our fingers.

As we sit there, time seems to slow. The rest of the world fades away, and it's just me and Holly, wrapped in our own private universe. With her hand in mine, I feel like I can take on anything the universe might throw at us.

She looks up at me with a smile. My eyes are drawn to her lips. When she moves closer to me, I know that she wants me to kiss her.

Though, I hesitate for a moment—unsure if she feels the same way. But then she licks her lips slightly, and all of my doubts fly away in an instant. My heart is pounding as I lean in towards her, and slowly, our lips touch for the first time.

The kiss is soft and sweet at first, then simmering. Our pulses quicken in anticipation. Then our kiss was like lightning. Sizzling and explosive. Passionate. Her lips are warm and inviting, and my cock has never been this hard from just a kiss. Taking her into my arms, I can feel her body responding to mine, and I know that she wants me just as badly as I want her.

We break apart, gasping for breath, and I look into her eyes. They are filled with a mixture of joy, desire, and uncertainty. Her mind is battling what she should do and what she wants. That's okay. I'm not going anywhere.

She may not know it yet, but she is mine. I know it one-hundred percent in my soul. With everything I am.

CHAPTER 6
HOLLY

FOR ONCE, it seems I'm the first one in the cabin awake. I take the time, lying in bed, and enjoy the silence. I can still feel Dean's lips on mine, sending shivers down my spine. I can hardly believe that we finally kissed. All day long, it was all I kept thinking about. It's as if my thoughts manifested it.

Finally, I decide to get up and make some coffee. As I walk into the kitchen, I see that Dean is already up and he's starting to cook breakfast. He's wearing only his jeans, and my eyes take in the broad width of his chest and the sculpted perfection of his abs. Just by looking at him, I feel myself getting turned on.

I try to keep my cool as I sit down at the table, but the sexual tension between us is palpable. Dean turns around and catches me looking at him. A sly grin spreads across his face as he leans in close to me.

"Good morning, beautiful," he whispers in my ear.

My heart races as I try to maintain my composure. His scent fills my senses, and I'm overwhelmed with the urge to kiss him again.

Even though I try to shake off the feeling and focus on making the coffee, Dean's presence is making it difficult. He easily moves around the kitchen, his muscles flexing as he flips the pancakes on the griddle. Once again, I'm admiring his physique, the way his broad shoulders taper down to his narrow waist and then widen again at his hips. It's like the gods forged him.

"Hey," he says, breaking me out of my reverie. "You okay there?"

I nod, trying to play it cool, but I know my face is flushed. "Yeah, I'm fine. Just enjoying the view." I try to flirt, but it has never really been my thing.

Dean chuckles and leans in closer to me. "I'll give you an even better view later," he says, giving me a playful wink and setting a cup of coffee on the table in front of me.

My heart rate increases at his words, and I can already feel myself getting wet between my legs.

"Mommy, I'm hungry," Gracie says before I get a chance to reply.

She walks over and crawls into my lap.

"Well, pancakes will be ready in just a few minutes," Dean says, and Gracie's face lights up with a huge smile.

Who knew a man making your kids smile like that was such a turn-on?

When I look up at Dean, he catches my gaze. We just stare into each other's eyes for a few moments before I have to look away. There's some electricity between us, and I know Dean feels it, too.

Max walks out just in time for us to enjoy the meal in comfortable silence. Even though I'm trying not to, I catch myself stealing glances at Dean as I sip my coffee. He keeps looking at me as well, which doesn't help the dampness between my legs.

Once the kids are dressed for the day and the kitchen is clean from breakfast, the kids want to know what the plan is for today.

"Well, this morning, I thought Max and I could go chop up some wood. We need to replenish our stash. Afterward, we can make some Christmas cookies and peppermint bark. What do you think?" "Yes, yes, yes!" The kids jump up and down.

"Alright, Max, go bundle up. Gracie, how about we do our nails? I have the pink polish you picked out last time," I say.

"Can I do your nails?" she asks.

"Of course."

I head to my room, grab the nail polish, and Dean and Max head outside.

While Gracie is doing my nails, she's chattering away about what kind of cookies we should make and how she plans to decorate hers. We have a great time together, and I make a note to do this more often. I need to make time for more one-on-one time with each of my kids.

After a few hours, Dean and Max return with an armful of wood they stack by the fireplace. We have a quick lunch and then get ready to bake Christmas cookies.

Dean takes the kids to gather ingredients from the pantry while I set up the cookie cutters, sprinkles, and frosting.

"Can we make some chocolate chip cookies with sprinkles too?" Max asks.

"You bet," I say, while Gracie and I prepare the dough.

The kitchen is filled with laughter and giggles as we make Christmas cookies and have some fun, stress-free time.

Dean wraps Gracie up in his arms as he shows her how to roll out the dough properly. She looks so content when he instructs her. Dean and I take turns helping the kids roll out cookie dough, cut them into holiday shapes, bake, and frost them.

Once we have made enough cookies to feed most of Mustang Mountain, we move on to making peppermint bark. This turns out to be just as much fun as baking cookies. We melt chocolate chips over the stove and spread them out on wax paper to cool. Once cooled, we decorate it with crushed candy canes and festive sprinkles. It looks almost too good to eat.

"Okay, go get cleaned up. We need to start preparing dinner. After dinner, we will decorate the Christmas tree!" Dean says, and the kids run off to get cleaned up.

Dinner flies by, as the kids talk about which of their cookies are their favorite. Our mealtime is fun and we all joke and laugh together. Whenever I steal glances at Dean throughout dinner, the electricity sizzles between us.

"Go change into your PJs and wash your hands and your face before we start on the tree," Dean says as we finish up dinner.

When the kids have gone, I stand in the kitchen and watch Dean clean up the mess. He turns to me, smirking, and says, "You know, I don't think I've ever had that much fun baking before." I laugh and blush a little, feeling his gaze on me.

"Me, neither," I agree.

Stepping closer, he places a hand on my waist and pulls me in close. I can feel the heat from his body as I move close to his magnificent chest.

He gently brushes his lips against mine. My heart flutters, and I close my eyes, enjoying the moment.

We stay like that for just a few minutes before finally pulling apart.

"Well, we should get going on decorating that tree," he whispers.

I nod, not trusting my voice, but follow him to the living room just as the kids come running in.

"Okay, first, we have to have some Christmas music." Dean heads over to the radio and pops in an old Christmas CD from the stack beside the bookcase. "Some good ole Johnny Cash Christmas should do it."

"Lights first!" Max says.

We spend the next few hours stringing up lights, and the kids pick out decorations for the tree. We all work together to hang the ornaments and decorations, and I marvel at how beautiful it looks.

Dean keeps finding little ways to brush my hand as we put up ornaments or to bump into me and give me a look, letting me know it was no accident.

They even have a stash of decorations that we place around the cabin. By the time everything is set up, it's past the kids' bedtime.

"Okay, guys, time for bed!" I say, and we tuck the kids in and read them a story before going to the living room to enjoy the glow of the Christmas tree. The thought that dominates my mind is how I don't have money to get the kids anything really nice for Christmas. I have no way of earning money right now, and I'm not even able to go out shopping for them.

I have to trust Dean's friends will figure things out, and hopefully, there is still time for me to come up with a plan.

"What a great day," Dean says as he sits down on the couch beside me, looking over at me and giving me a gentle smile.

"It was," I agree.

He takes my hand in his, and I scoot closer to him, laying my head on his shoulder. Taking a deep breath, I fill my lungs with the scent of wood burning in the fireplace.

"I'm thankful for days like this," he says, his arms wrapping around me and holding me close.

"Me, too," I murmur.

Sighing, I take this moment in, thankful for all the sweet memories we made together today.

"Would you like something to drink?" Dean asks, breaking the comfortable silence.

"Sure," I say.

Standing, goes into the kitchen and returns with two glasses of spiked apple cider. Handing me a glass, he says, "You will have a hard time throwing a stick and not finding spiked apple cider here in Mustang Mountain."

We sit in silence as we sip our drinks, and the warmth from the cider spreads through my body. Dean slowly moves closer to me, his arm wrapping around me and his hand gently stroking my side. Loving the feeling of his strong arms around me, I move even closer.

Dean looks down at me with a twinkle in his eyes and leans in, gently kissing me on the forehead before pressing his lips against mine.

Our kiss deepens, his tongue slipping into my mouth and exploring every inch. I let out a small moan, feeling my own desire build within me. His hands move down to my waist, pulling me even closer to him. I can feel the growing hardness in his pants against my thigh, and I know he wants me just as badly as I want him.

Breaking the kiss, he whispers, "Let's take this to the bedroom."

Nodding, I stand, following him to his bedroom. He lays me down on the bed and joins me, pulling me into his arms. We kiss, and he moves his hands slowly, caressing me over my hips and up my back, though he doesn't make a move to remove my clothes.

All I want is to feel him skin-to-skin, so I slip my hand under his shirt and move it up his chest. But then he stops me by taking my hand. Bringing my hand up to his mouth, he places a kiss in the center of it.

"I'm not sleeping with you tonight because you have been drinking. When I finally sink into you, I want you to remember every detail."

Feeling my cheeks heat up, I allow the thoughts of throwing caution to the wind to pass through me. He is taking this seriously, and in that moment, I know he is serious about us being together. That alone excites me even more. And I'm already burning hot.

Even though I try to change my thoughts and relieve some of the pressure building in my core, the feel of the fabric pressing on my pussy only makes things worse.

"You're turned on, aren't you?" he whispers, watching me.

When I nod, his breathing picks up.

"Do you want me to make you come, baby?" he says, and again, I nod.

Trailing his hand down my stomach and under my black leggings, I am an inch away from coming.

"Are you sure?" he asks, letting his finger feather over my clit.

Moaning, I cry out, "Yes, oh god, yes..."

Sensuously, he moves his finger in teasing circles, alternating between subtle touches and more aggressive ones.

Then he leans down and kisses me, catching my moans as they grow louder.

"Harder.... Please!" I beg.

He does as I ask, pushing me closer and closer to the edge.

"That's it, let it go," he whispers in my ear, and I do. His mouth is on me again, stopping me from screaming out his name as pleasure overwhelms me.

When I'm finally able to catch my breath, he pulls back, looking at me with satisfaction. Then he places a soft kiss on my lips. We lie there for some time in silence until I am able to get myself together again to cuddle up against him.

"Thank you," I whisper in his ear, feeling grateful for what he just did.

"Anytime, sweetheart," he whispers back, and I smile, feeling content and exhausted simultaneously.

CHAPTER 7
DEAN

FUCK. I'm having the most amazing dream of finally making love to Holly. Only my dreams are never this hot. They never have every nerve of mine on fire. My eyes shoot open, only to find the sexiest scene before me that almost has me coming on the spot.

Holly is between my legs, with her mouth wrapped around my cock. Her eyes lock with mine, and only then does she slide my cock from her mouth and smile.

"I still want you," she says, shyly.

Fuck if it isn't sexy. Flipping her on her back so I'm caging her in, I pull her up to my mouth and kiss her hard. Then I cup her generous rosy-nippled breasts before trailing down her stomach over her luscious curves, and slip under her leggings, finding her soaking wet.

"Fuck, look how wet you got sucking my cock." When I start playing with her, she whimpers. "You have to be quiet, so we don't wake the kids because once I'm inside you, I'm not stopping for anything. The house can burn down around us, but I won't stop," I threaten.

My cock is already throbbing and wet, and I can't wait to be inside her. Before removing her clothes, I lock the door. Then I take off my clothes and grab a condom. I roll it on as I walk back over to the bed and take in the goddess lying naked on my bed, right where she belongs.

She watches me with hooded eyes. I kneel in front of her, spread her legs wide and slide my cock inside her tight pussy. We both moan, and then she wraps her legs around my waist as I push into her.

Every nerve is on fire as I keep her eyes locked with mine, thrusting into her. The feeling of her tightness consumes me, and I'm lost in it. Moving slowly, I give her time to adjust, but I want to move fast and hard.

I'm panting, trying to hold back, but I can feel Holly's orgasm build. Moving faster, I'm lost in the feeling of how tight and wet she is. Then she bites my shoulder, and I realize she's coming.

My own orgasm builds, and I thrust in faster and faster, knowing that when I come, it's going to be explosive.

She captures my mouth with hers as I move faster and harder, and I'm about to go over when I feel her tensely grip my arms and scream my name into our kiss. She gifts me with another orgasm.

It's the most beautiful sound I've ever heard, and I know I'm home. Finally, I give in, and with a final thrust into her, I cum harder than I ever have before.

I collapse beside her, never wanting this moment to end.

"You're so fucking sexy, Holly. I love you." Those words slip out before I even realize it.

She looks at me with tears in her eyes, kissing me softly.

"I love you, too," she says.

We lie there holding each other, and I feel like I'm exactly where I'm supposed to be. "I didn't know I could feel this much for someone so fast," she says.

"Ruby, the Mayor's wife, has been on the crusade to match up the single guys in town. So, this year several of my buddies have fallen in love. They were always talking about how hard they fell and certainly, when they weren't expecting it. I didn't think love was in the cards for me until I met you. Seeing you that first day back at the shelter hit me hard," I admit.

We lie there in silence a bit longer, and I decide to go for broke.

"I want to marry you and be a family."

She shoots up, pulling the sheet over her, and looks at me with amazement. "What did you say?"

"I want to marry you, Holly. I want to be the father to your kids. I can't imagine my life without you or them in it. Please say yes." I look deep into her eyes.

When she cries and nods her head, I pull her as close as I can get her to me and hold her tight.

"Yes, yes, I'll marry you."

Not ever wanting to move out of her arms, I kiss her passionately. I can't believe it! I'm finally getting my chance at having a family.

Immediately, we start making plans.

"My cabin has four bedrooms and an office. It's more than double the size of this one. So, it will fit all your stuff," I tell her.

"I sold pretty much everything. All we have is what we brought with us," she says quietly.

"Then we can head into Whitefish to shop for whatever you and the kids need. I'm sure they will want to decorate their own rooms however they want. That can be part of their Christmas gifts."

"As soon as it's safe, I'll start looking for a job," she says.

I can hear her mind racing from here. "First off, there is no rush. I make plenty of money as a software developer and have plenty of money saved because of a big project I worked on a few years ago. You don't have to work if you don't want to. If you choose to work, I want it to be something you love doing, and you can even volunteer if it's just about getting out of the house and meeting people."

"I guess we can figure it out if we are ever able to leave this cabin," she sighs.

I tilt her chin to look up at me. "We will be able to leave, and soon. I trust the other Riders as if they are my own brothers. Plus, Six is the Secretary, one of the higher-ups. He won't let this slip past anyone. My guess is there isn't a single club member without some kind of job to end this as we speak."

"I hope you're right. I don't know how much longer we can distract the kids before they start asking questions about why we can't go into town."

Kissing her forehead, I hug her tight. "Yeah, I don't want to be the one to have to tell them we aren't safe right now, either."

"You are plenty safe. It's me and them at risk," she says.

"Sweetheart, you just agreed to be mine. It's us. There is no you anymore, or you and the kids. It's the kids and us. I'm in this for the long haul, and I'm not going anywhere."

She relaxes in my arms and nods her head. For a moment, we simply look at each other, letting the gravity of my words sink in.

"What are The Mustang Mountain Riders like? What does it mean to be the wife of a member?"

"It means you have a family who will fight for you, take care of you and the kids, and give you the safest possible life. As for the Riders, we are a brotherhood, but we can also be fiercely protective. For the Riders, family comes first."

I go on, "The Mustang Mountain Riders are the good guys. We are always doing charity rides and helping people in need. Sometimes we do rides to get women out of bad situations and to the safety of the shelter. If we can help the community, we do. The other wives will welcome you with open arms. Instantly, you'll have more friends than you will know what to do with."

We lay there for what feels like hours, talking and planning for our future together. I know this is only the start of a beautiful life for us all, and I can't wait to begin.

"I think I want to volunteer sometime at the women's shelter. It brought me you, and I want to help other women get out of situations like I was in," she says as the room fills with sunlight.

"I think that's a great idea. Courtney will be grateful for your help, I'm sure."

She smiles at me, and I can tell she is feeling more and more secure in this plan.

"Yeah, maybe that's why I had to go through what I did. So, I could find you and then go on to help other women in need."

"I know you'll be able to help them. Whatever happens, I'm here for you. Bottom line, eventually you'll find strength in the Riders. It's a family, not just a club," I remind her.

She snuggles closer, and I kiss her head. I'm so relaxed with her that we start drifting off to sleep again.

Only we aren't woken up by the kid's laughter or them calling out for their mom. Pounding on the front door wakes us up.

CHAPTER 8
HOLLY

MY HEART RACES at hearing the pounding at the door. Quickly, Dean and I move to get our clothes on.

"Go sit with the kids. I'll get the door." Dean grabs a shotgun from a shelf above his bedroom door.

I go into the kids' room, closing the door behind me.

"Mommy, who is at the door? Is it Grandma?" Gracie asks.

"No, it's not Grandma. I'm not sure who it is, but Dean is going to go check. Let's stay here until we know who it is."

As I sit with the kids, my mind races with possibilities of who could be at the door. Dean says only his mom, dad, and brother know where the cabin is. But what are the chances the guys from Savage Bones found it?

No, that can't be. They wouldn't be knocking on the door. They'd just bust in, not caring about anyone or anything.

The door opens, and there is some muffled talking before Dean calls out. "Holly, sweetheart, it's my brother."

Instant relief fills me. I hear the sound of boots stomping on the wooden floor as Dean and Six make their way to the living room. Trying to make myself more presentable, I run my fingers through my hair before the kids and I go out to greet him.

"Why don't you and the kids get dressed? There is plenty of snow for the kids to build a snowman while we talk," Six says.

His meaning is clear. What he has to say isn't meant for the kids to hear. In my heart, I know it's an update on Savage Bones, and judging by the fact there isn't even a hint of a smile on his face, it's not good news.

"Okay, kids, let's get your clothes on so we can make a snowman while the weather is nice!"

My heart sinks as I watch the kids pull their coats on while Dean and Six huddle in the living room. I know what this means. It means the danger is closer than we thought.

But I can't think about that right now. I have to focus on keeping the kids happy and calm. Grabbing a few granola bars, I hand one to each of them before they run out into the snow.

Dean, Six, and I stay back on the porch, watching them for a moment when Six speaks.

"We found your stepdad. Not so much as found him as he made his presence known," Six says, making my heart sink.

Dean steps up behind me and wraps his arms around me.

"What does that mean?" I ask, my voice shaky.

Six turns to me, his eyes hard. "It means he showed up back at your mom's house. Our best guess is when she didn't know where you were, things turned ugly."

I feel sick to my stomach. "Ugly how?" I'm almost too scared to ask.

Six looks over me to Dean, who pulls me tight against him.

"He beat your mom up pretty bad. She's in the hospital unconscious," Six says.

When my knees give out, Dean slowly lowers me to the ground.

"We won't let him anywhere near you," Dean vows, but I barely hear him.

The tears are streaming down my face as my mind tries to process the news. My mom, the one person who has always been there for me, is lying in a hospital bed because of that monster, because of me. Rage and sadness fill my heart, making it hard to breathe.

"Your stepdad got away before the police arrived. We don't know where he is now, but we're trying to track him down." Six's voice is calm, but I can hear the underlying anger and determination.

"It should be me in the hospital bed." I speak the truth because he was after me, but found my mom instead.

"Don't you dare say that! This is your stepdad's fault. Also, your mom knew what kind of guy he was and chose to stay. You knew what kind of guy he was and chose to protect your kids. Even though I know it doesn't feel like it, you made the right choice," Six says.

"Holly, this is not your fault," Dean says firmly, as if he can sense my thoughts. "You couldn't have known this was going to happen."

Though I nod my head in agreement, my mind feels muddled with thoughts and emotions.

Six chimes in, "We're going to find him. And we're going to make sure he pays for what he did to your mom. We won't stop until he's behind bars."

Dean squeezes me tighter, his warmth providing a small sense of comfort amidst the chaos. "We'll keep you safe, Holly. That's a promise."

Taking a deep breath, I wipe my tears with the sleeve of my jacket. "Thank you," I say quietly,

70

grateful for the support of these two men who have become my family.

But despite their promises, I know that the danger is still out there. My stepdad, a man who has always been abusive, is now more dangerous than ever.

"I need to be there. I need to be with my mom. I need to be there if she..." I get choked up and can't find the words to say if she doesn't make it, but they seem to get what I'm trying to say.

"You can't right now. It's not safe. We'll take you to your mom as soon as we catch your stepdad. Some of the guys think he did this to try to flush you out, thinking you'll rush to your mom's side," Six says.

I nod in understanding, feeling a mix of guilt and fear for not being able to be there for my mom.

"Then use me as bait. Let me go see my mom and flush him out," I say the moment the idea pops into my head.

"Absolutely not," Six and Dean say at the same time.

At their protective instincts, I can feel my frustration rising.

"I just want to see her," I whisper, more to myself than anyone else.

Dean cups my face in his hands, forcing me to look at him. "We'll find him, Holly. And we'll make sure you get to see your mother. But we need to be smart about this. We have to work together and stay safe."

"Right now, we don't know if Savage Bones is in on this, too, or if your stepdad is working alone. We haven't been able to figure it out. If Savage Bones is involved, then this is a bigger trap than we thought. If they're trying to make sure you don't talk, you won't make it inside the hospital alive," Six says.

"But I have you guys to protect me."

"Using yourself as bait is not an option," Dean says firmly.

While I understand where they're coming from, the thought of my mom lying in the hospital alone, fighting for her life, is too much to bear. I want to be there for her and tell her that I love her, and that everything will be okay.

I can't help feeling as if I'm trapped, helpless in this situation. The thought of not being able to see my mother is tearing me apart.

"This is my fault, so it's up to me to make it right. It's not right to put this all on your shoulders," I try again.

"Holly. You just agreed to marry me. That means yes, what you are dealing with is the club's problem," Dean says.

"Damn, brother. You could have opened with that when I got here. Congratulations to you two," Six says, resting a hand on my shoulder. "Dean is right. Even more so now. It's not just that he was threatening someone who lives in Mustang Mountain. He's now threatening a member of the Riders, our family. We don't allow that."

"Plus, you have to protect your children. You're all they have until we are married, and I can legally adopt them. What happens to them if something happens to you?" Dean asks.

Six intervenes. "The guys are meeting now to come up with a plan, but I knew as soon as I heard about your mom, I needed to come tell you since there is no phone service out here. I'll be back once we have a plan in place. For now, stay here. This is where you are safest. Do you need me to bring back anything?"

"Some more groceries. We are good for now, but those kids eat a lot when they are burning energy out in the snow like this."

Dean is speaking, and I hear him, but I feel like I'm somewhere else completely.

When Six leaves, Dean takes my hand and leads me to the couch. Before we call for the kids to come inside, Dean's arms hold me close, and I try to calm my racing thoughts.

"I'm scared, Dean," I confess. "What if we can't find him? What if he comes after us?"

"We won't let that happen," he says firmly. "We're going to find him, Holly. And we're going to make sure he can never hurt you or our family again."

Leaning my head against his chest, I listen to the steady thump of his heartbeat. For a moment, it's enough to forget about the danger lurking outside, the uncertainty of our future, and the fear consuming me.

As my mind races, I wonder if The Mustang Mountain Riders know how strong and how brutal the Savage Bones really are. How will a bunch of nice guys take them down and protect me and my kids?

CHAPTER 9

HOLLY

THE LAST TIME I felt this helpless was when I watched my husband die of cancer, knowing there was nothing I could do about it. Now my mom is lying in a hospital bed, broken and bloody because of me, and I can't even be there to tell her she isn't alone and how much I love her.

I know she needs a little extra encouragement to pull through. My mom has always been the kind of person who needs extra strength from time to time. When I was growing up, I was always happy to give it to her.

Now, I can't be there for her, and it's killing me. I know I need to keep my kids safe, and they are, especially here in the cabin with Dean. He's agreed to take us on as a family. The kids love him and feel protected with him. But we won't ever be safe and able to leave this mountain if we don't take care of my stepdad.

Needing to get out of the cabin, I walk down from the porch to the edge of the woods behind the cabin. I can see the smoke from the chimney coming out of the rusted metal roof, and for a moment, I close my eyes and cling to the hope that we can still have a normal life. That we can live in the same cabin and have Christmas dinners, and the kids can run around the snow and make snowmen every year.

Taking a deep breath, I steel myself for what I have to do. Dean is out chopping wood, and the kids are playing outside near him. It's just me and my thoughts as I head back into the cabin, and I can't let fear get the best of me. I know where my stepdad is. He's waiting for me to show up at the hospital, and I know what I have to do to keep my family safe.

I grab a piece of paper and write a letter no mom ever wants to. Then I write two other letters, one to each of my kids, and I stash them under the mattress out of sight, and go out to join Dean and the kids.

As I approach Dean, I can sense his gaze fixated on me. He knows something's up. It's easy to see that he's worried about the situation and about me. He drops his ax and walks towards me, and as he does, I can feel my heart rate quickening. I take another deep breath, trying to control my emotions.

He wraps his arms around my waist and bends his knees to lower his body so he can look into my eyes. It's as if he's able to read everything without me having to say a word. I expect some questions or for him to say everything is going to be okay.

Instead, he picks me up and swings me around. My heart rate accelerates. The motion is exhilarating, and I can feel the wind rushing past me. When I start laughing, the kids join in, laughing even harder. Dean then swings me over his shoulder and starts running towards the kids, roaring as loud as he can. They run away, giggling happily.

Right then, I forget about my stepdad and the danger that we are in. The moment is so pure and carefree, something we haven't experienced in a long time. When he sets me back down, he even has a big smile lighting his face. It takes my breath away how handsome he really is, especially when he smiles like this.

If we make it out of this together, I vow to myself to do anything and everything I can to put that smile on his face more often. Dean pulls me to his side as we watch the kids. Gracie fights off a yawn, and Max is starting to wind down, too.

"How about lunch and then a family nap time? Even I'm tired after all that," I say. There is very little protesting.

We make grilled cheese with some tomato soup to warm everyone up, and the lunchtime debate topic is what Christmas movie we are going to watch tonight. By the end of lunch, we have landed on watching *The Grinch* after dinner.

As we finish cleaning up after lunch, I feel Dean's hand on my back, gently rubbing up and down. It's a subtle motion but fills me with comfort. We've only known each other for a short time, but it feels like we've been through so much together. His touch sends shivers down my spine, and I know that I'm not the only one who feels the attraction between us.

"Go tuck the kids in. I'll finish up here," he says, leaning in to kiss me quickly.

After letting the kids pick out a book, I tuck them in tight, giving them each an extra hug and kiss. I read them the book they picked, and both are asleep before I even get to the halfway point.

As I step out of the kids' room, I cannot shake off the anxiety that has been gnawing at me all day long. Dean is leaning against the door frame to his bedroom with his arms folded across his chest. When I make a move to walk past him, he blocks me with his body, making me face him. My heartbeat picks up again, and I can feel my face flush as my eyes meet his.

"Are you okay?" he asks, his voice laced with concern.

I nod, but I'm pretty sure he can tell I'm lying. He reaches out and tucks a strand of hair behind my ear. That simple act of caring makes me feel vulnerable.

"Just worried about Mom and what is going to happen with my stepdad," I tell him as honestly as I can.

He pulls me into him and rests his forehead on mine. "I'm not going to let anything happen to you or our family. We'll face it together," he whispers back, his breath tickling my ear.

While I want to believe him, I can't shake off the feeling that something is wrong. My stepdad's threats are still ringing in my ears, and I have an overwhelming fear that we're in danger. Dean's touch is so comforting that I let myself relax against him for a minute.

"Let's lie down. I wasn't kidding about needing a nap today, too," I say.

He pulls me into the room, helping me into bed and holding me tight.

I soak in the feeling of being in his arms.

As we lie there, I feel the tension in my body slowly seeping away. Dean's embrace is like a warm cocoon, protecting me from the outside world. I can hear his heart beating in my ears, and I am lulled into a sense of calmness. The sun is shining through the curtains, casting a warm glow across the room.

It's not long before his grip on me loosens, and his breathing evens out. I wait a bit, letting him get into a deep sleep before I gently move his arms to slide out of bed. Placing my pillow in his arms, I quietly leave the room, closing the bedroom door behind me.

Taking the letters I wrote out from under my mattress, I lay them on top of my bed. Then I go to the kitchen, grab the food I put to the side earlier, and pack it with some water in a backpack I brought from the shelter. I get all bundled up in several layers, and put on my heavy jacket and boots.

I take one last look around, knowing I have to do this. To make us all safe, I have to put an end to this.

When I go outside, there is a fresh layer of snow on the ground from last night. But the sun is bright and offers a bit of warmth.

As I walk through the snow-covered path toward the gravel road that leads to the cabin, my heart is beating faster. My stepdad's threats keep repeating in my mind. I can't let him harm us, and I have to do whatever it takes to protect my family.

If I can follow the road down the mountain, once closer to town, I can get a ride. I have plenty of daylight left, and the sun shining makes the walk beautiful.

As I venture further into the woods, the sky grows darker, and a snowstorm pops up from what seems like thin air. All of a sudden, I can't see the road and don't know if I'm even walking in the right direction anymore.

The snow is falling at a steady pace and has covered pretty much everything in white. The snowflakes dance around me, getting heavier with each passing minute. Soon, the trees are completely covered in white, making it almost impossible to see the path ahead of me. The wind is howling through the treetops, and cold air penetrates all my layers of clothing, chilling me to my core.

I have no idea which direction I should take next, and fear grips me from within, making it hard to breathe. I feel like I'm in a dream and want to wake up. Turning, I head back to the cabin, figuring I can follow my footsteps. Yet in only a few minutes, my footprints disappear in the snow.

I keep walking in what I hope is the right direction, but my strength is quickly draining away. My vision blurs, and my steps become wobbly. I stop for a moment to catch my breath and rest against a tree, trying to gather all my remaining energy and focus it on returning home.

A gust of wind howls past me, lifting the snow from the ground and making it hard to see anything ahead of me. With no idea where I am going, I know that if I don't get back soon, things could turn really bad for me.

Even though I try to keep going, I can't feel my hands and feet anymore, and with each step forward, it's harder and harder to stay aware. Then my foot hits a branch and I let out a yell that is swallowed up by the wind. My vision starts to go blurry, and just before it goes black, a grey wolf crosses what is left of my vision.

"Hades..." I croak out just before everything goes black.

CHAPTER 10
DEAN

ONCE AGAIN, I'm woken up by pounding on the door. I roll over and reach for Holly, only to find a cold, empty bed. She must have gotten up with the kids and let me sleep.

I smile because family nap time is definitely one of my favorite family activities. I get up and head to the door. As I pass the kids' room, I see they are still asleep and then find the living room empty.

Where the heck is Holly?

I open the door to find my brother on the other side.

"A snowstorm came out of nowhere on my way up the mountain. I might be stuck here for the night. But I wanted to come update you," he says.

"Come in, let me go find Holly." I head back to the bedroom, thinking maybe she's in the bathroom.

But as I pass her room, something catches my eye. Papers on her bed. I go in and pick them up, seeing my name on the top one.

Dean,

I'm sorry.

I can't let my mother sit in that hospital all alone and allow my stepdad to keep threatening my kids.

83

While I know the risk I am taking, I also know my kids couldn't be safer than with you.

If my stepdad needs to have me to keep them safe, then I will do it. I leave my kids with you. Everything of mine is yours. When I agreed to marry you, I did it with my whole heart.

I just know we can't keep living like this, so I'm putting an end to it.

When I said I love you, I meant it.

You and the kids are everything to me.

Holly

My heart drops as I read Holly's words. I can feel the panic rising in my chest as I try to process what I'm reading. She's gone. She left me and the kids behind.

"Fuck!" I say and rush back to the living room. "Holly's gone. She left to go see her mom." I hold up the letter.

"Your truck is still in the driveway," he says with a confused look.

"She can't drive a stick. She would have gone on foot." I start rushing around to pull on my clothes and jackets.

"In this weather?" Six asks.

"When we laid down to take a nap, it was bright and sunny. We had no idea a snowstorm was on its

84

way. I have to go after her. The kids will be waking up any minute. I don't know what to tell them, but don't let on that anything is wrong." I say, grabbing a shotgun, compass, and GPS tracker so my brother can find me if needed.

"Be safe. You have one hour before I load the kids up and come after you," he says.

No sooner than I step off the front porch, Hades comes running out of the forest. He starts howling as soon as he sees me.

"Did you find her, boy? You know where she is?" I rush toward him.

He walks back into the woods, only stopping to look back at me to make sure I'm following. He keeps a steady, fast pace, and I'm struggling to keep up over the brush and fallen trees.

As I follow Hades deeper into the forest, the snowfall becomes lighter, but the wind picks up. My breaths come out in quick puffs as I trudge through the deep snow, following the wolf's lead. I shiver, my fingers and toes already starting to feel numb despite the thick layers I'm wearing.

Making my way through the snow behind Hades, all I can think of is Holly. My mind is racing, trying to piece together what could have made her leave. Was it really just her mother's injuries and her stepdad's threats? Or was there something else going on that I wasn't aware of? I shake my head, trying to clear my thoughts. Right now, I need to focus on finding her first and asking questions later.

Hades suddenly stops, sniffing the air. I pause, too, listening for any sounds that might indicate where Holly is. Hades turns to glance at me before barking and running off to the left.

I follow, fear and worry gripping my heart. If we find Holly, I can only hope that everything will turn out okay. I think of the future I had planned with her and all the dreams we had for our family.

He stops once again, this time letting out a low growl. I look ahead in the direction he's facing, and my breath catches in my throat. There, barely visible through the trees, is Holly, slouched against a tree.

I rush to her side, only to find her unconscious. Anxiously, I check her, and thankfully, she has a pulse, but it's weak. I pull out the thick blanket from my pack and wrap her in it before picking her up and turning to Hades.

"Okay, boy, I need you to lead us back home," I say, trying not to let the panic fill my voice. I can't do anything for her out here.

Hades barks in agreement and leads the way back through the forest, with me cradling Holly in my arms. The wind picks up, making navigating through the heavy snow more difficult. I focus all my energy on keeping Holly safe and warm while following Hades' lead.

Holding Holly tightly to my chest, I pray she'll make it through. I can feel the weight of her body as I trudge through the snow, and I do my best to keep my footing.

"Dean," Holly sighs at one point, but her eyes are still closed.

"Holly, stay with me. We are almost back in the cabin and then we'll warm you up. Stay with me, Holly. I love you, baby. I can't do this without you." I try to pour all my emotions into my words to let her know what she really means to me.

"I love you, too, Dean," she says as her head rolls to the side.

With every fiber of my being, I have to believe that she heard me and that she is fighting for me, for us, the best way she can.

I feel a sense of relief wash over me as we finally arrive back at the cabin. Hades starts howling as we break the tree line, and Six comes rushing out.

"She's unconscious. We need to get her warm," I say as he holds the door for me.

"Take her to the bedroom, strip her down and you strip, too. Get both of you under the blankets. I'll find some extra blankets and the heated blanket mom keeps here," he orders.

Doing as he says and closing the bedroom door behind me, I lay Holly down on the bed and start to remove her wet clothes, my hands shaking with worry. With each layer of clothing stripped away from her, my heart races. She's cold to the touch.

I undress as quickly as possible, clumsily fumbling with the buttons and zippers. When I'm down to my underwear, I crawl into bed beside her and pull the blankets over us. It's only a matter of moments until Six comes in with more blankets and the heated one.

"Let's put the heated blanket on and then the others over you. You'll start sweating, but she needs the heat," he says, spreading the blanket out and plugging it in.

"I don't care. I just need her to be okay." I pull her into my arms, offering her as much body heat as possible.

As I hold Holly close to me, I can feel the warmth slowly returning to her body. While I know we're not out of the woods yet, at least she's safe and alive. Six sits in a chair beside the bed, watching us. He looks worried, his hands fidgeting in his lap.

"You did well, Dean. You found her in time," Six says, breaking the silence.

I nod, not trusting myself to speak. I'm still shaking with fear and adrenaline.

"I don't know what I would do without her," I say, my voice cracking. "I can't imagine a future without her in it."

Six nods, but I know he won't get it until he falls ass over heels for a woman someday.

"The kids?" I ask, not wanting them to see their mom like this.

"They were in their room coloring when you came in. I set them up with a Christmas movie and cookies. Gave Hades a few cookies, too. He's camping out on the front porch."

I don't know how long we lie there, but eventually, Holly stirs in my arms, her eyelids fluttering open. I lean in close, my heart pounding in my chest. "Holly?" I whisper.

She blinks up at me, her eyes unfocused. "Dean?" she murmurs, her voice hoarse.

I stroke her hair gently, relief flooding through me. "Yeah, baby, it's me," I whisper. "You scared me."

She tries to sit up, but I hold her still. "Don't move too much," I caution. "You've been out for a while. How are you feeling?"

Holly winces as she tries to move, a pained expression crossing her face. "I'm so cold," she says, shivering.

I lean in and kiss her forehead. "We're working on getting you warm," I promise her, smoothing her hair back from her face.

Six stands up from his chair. "I'll go get you some warm soup and hot tea," he says, glancing at Holly. "You both need to eat and stay hydrated."

As he exits the room, Holly looks up at me, her eyes filled with gratitude. "I don't know what would have happened if you didn't find me," she whispers, her voice weak.

I hold her tighter, bringing her closer to my chest. "I'll always find you," I say, my voice firm. "I won't let anything happen to you."

Our mouths meet in a slow, tender kiss, and for a moment, everything else fades away. The only thing that matters is the two of us, together, safe and warm, in this cabin in the mountains. As we break apart, Holly leans her head against my chest. I feel her body relax against mine, her breathing slowing down. Within moments, she's asleep again, her body warming up from the heated blanket.

I let her rest until Six comes back with some soup, and he sits on the bed beside me.

"Hey man, grab my sweatshirt off the dresser for me. She can wear it when she sits up," I say.

He hands it to me, and then leaves, closing the door behind him.

"Holly, baby. Time to sit up and eat some soup while it's hot." I wake her gently.

She stirs, opening her eyes.

"Here, sit up, put this sweatshirt on, and let's get some soup in you. Looks like some hot chocolate and water, too."

Holly sits, wrapping the sweatshirt around herself. I help her settle back against the pillows and hand her a spoonful of soup. She eats slowly. Her appetite is still weak, but I'm grateful that she's eating at all. As she finishes the soup, I give her the cup of hot chocolate. She takes a small sip, savoring the warmth.

"Thank you," she murmurs, looking up at me with soft eyes.

I smile down at her, my heart swelling with love. "Anything for you, Holly. You mean everything to me."

We chat quietly, the mood lightening as Holly's strength returns. We have a lot to talk about, like why she left. But for now, I'm just happy she is back and safe.

CHAPTER 11
HOLLY

WHEN DEAN SAYS he will make something happen, I've learned in the last forty-eight hours that he will move mountains to make it happen. He and his brother worked with other members of The Mustang Mountain Riders to make sure I was safe to visit my mom in the hospital and that my kids were protected while I was gone as well. He said he would do anything for his family. So, my kids and I are now his family.

Ace and Everly will stay with the kids since Ace has a military background. Mack and Lily will be there, too. Mack was a firefighter, so he has an EMT background, and Lily is making gingerbread houses with the kids since she is an amazing cook and baker.

Courtney talked to me and gave her approval for all four of them. While all this is going on, Jensen and Courtney are locking down the women's shelter to be safe.

While I'm walking in the hospital with Dean, Six and a huge man who introduces himself as Bear, I'm told that there are no less than two dozen Mustang Mountain Riders' eyes on us and the hospital. In addition, there are several more undercover law enforcement officers placed around the hospital.

I met Bear for the first time today, and it's easy to see why they call him Bear. He's tall, large, and made of muscle. Every bit of his arms I can see are covered in tattoos, and his face says "fuck around and find out" pretty much all the time.

As we enter the hospital, I can feel the nervousness bubbling inside me. It's been a while since I've seen my mom, and I don't know what to expect. Dean senses my anxiety and slips his hand into mine, squeezing it reassuringly. I look up at him and find comfort in how calm he is and how he is taking charge.

Bear and Six flank us as we make our way to my mother's room. I'm so grateful for their protection. Mustang Mountain might be a small town nestled in the mountains, but it's not immune to danger, and these men have connections even all the way up here in Whitefish. Bear walks with purpose, occasionally nodding at the other Riders we pass.

We make it all the way to my mom's room without any sign of my stepdad or any hint of Savage Bones. Though I worry that we won't end this today, and I will still be on pins and needles for weeks, months and possibly years. Trying ignore that thought, I decide to put my trust in the other Mustang Mountain Riders, as Dean has.

Before walking in, I pause at the door to my mom's room. I'm not sure what awaits me on the other side. Bear steps in first and does a sweep of the room and attached bathroom before nodding to us.

"I'll let a nurse know you are here and want to be updated on your mom," Six says, heading towards the nurses' station.

"I'll stay at the door," Bear says, crossing his arms and looking very much like some hired security guy.

Walking into the hospital room with Dean at my side, I see my mom lying on the bed, her skin sallow and her breathing labored. She has black eyes and cuts on her cheek and lip. The sight makes my heart ache, and tears prick at my eyes. I take a deep breath and step forward, reaching out to take her hand.

"Hi, Mom," my voice is barely above a whisper.

When her eyes flutter open, I gasp. The last time we heard, she was unconscious, and we hadn't been told otherwise. Thankfully, this is also when the doctor and nurse walk in.

"Is this your daughter?" The doctor asks Mom, who just nods, never taking her eyes off me.

"Can I let her know of your condition?" he asks, and again she nods.

"Okay, first, we have been notified her husband did this to her, and he has been barred from all information and visiting her. Until last night, she was in a medically induced coma. We wanted to give her some time to heal. She has a few cracked ribs, a broken arm, and a sprained ankle. In addition, she had to have surgery to remove several glass shards from her upper thigh and arm. She has close to seventy stitches in several places on her body, along with many bruises and small surface scratches." The doctor continues, reading the chart.

"She is very lucky, as far as the cases I've seen like this. We'd like to keep her here for several more days to make sure everything is healing right and there is no infection or side effects from the coma. After she's discharged, she will need a safe place to go. We will have her meet with a counselor, and they will tell her even if the person who did this is locked up, she should find a safe place that isn't her house to stay. In addition, we recommend that she press charges." The doctor stops and looks at us.

"That won't be a problem. We have a safe place for her to stay," Dean says, shaking the doctor's hand.

The nurse finishes checking her vitals and asks about her pain level.

"Holly, who is this man?" My mom asks, in a barely there, shaky voice.

"This is... well, this is my fiancé, Dean," I say proudly, looking over at Dean.

His smile could light up Las Vegas all on his own, and he squeezes my hand.

"You didn't tell me you were seeing anyone," Mom says with a small smile.

"Well, there will be plenty of time for sharing all the details," I say, then take another good look at my mom with tears in my eyes. "Oh, Mom, this is all my fault." I lean in and hug her.

"Nonsense. You hear me? I knew what kind of man he was, and I stayed. I didn't know how to leave. I thought it was the best way to keep you safe. Speaking of, you know this is a trap, right? As soon as you leave here, he's going to make a grab for you or follow you." My mom starts to panic.

"Actually, he won't. Ford, Jackson, and Owen just caught him. The police apprehended a few of the lower thugs Savage Bones was using as muscle, too. The rest of the club scattered as soon as they saw us." Bear peeks his head in to give us the news.

"She's still in danger from the other Savage Bones guys, though, isn't she?" I ask.

"Yeah, but Priest, Stone, and I are taking shifts. Someone will be with her around the clock until she is released," Bear says.

"Why would Savage Bones be worried about you guys?" My mom asks, sitting up slightly.

"Well, Dean and his buddies here are part of The Mustang Mountain Riders," I say.

Her eyes widen. "You are trading trouble, young lady," she says in as stern of a voice as she can manage.

"Mom, Savage Bones is a one-percent club. The Mustang Mountain Riders? They're good guys. They have been protecting me and the kids and the town."

"What is a one-percent club?" Mom asks.

"They are the one percent of motorcycle clubs that think they are above the law. They have no moral code, and they are heavily into illegal things. Drugs, guns, sex trade," Dean says.

"The Mustang Mountain Riders help pull women from abusive situations," I say. They help anyone who needs it, even animals. Lily told me about how they banded together to save a wild Mustang this spring and a litter abandoned kitten a few months ago. They are going to help you, too, Mom. We have a safe place for you to recuperate."

Mom won't make eye contact with me, and I know something is up.

"You are pressing charges and leaving, right, Mom?"

"I... don't know. Maybe it's better we all just forget about this," she says, waving her hands in front of her.

97

I look at Dean, and I can tell he's worried. He leans in and whispers in my ear. "If she doesn't press charges, they can't hold him, and he will be released," he says, and a cold chill races through me.

"Mom, look at me," I say, waiting until her eyes are on me. "If you don't press charges and he goes free, all this is for nothing. If he goes free, the kids and I aren't safe, and we can't stay here, which means you won't see your grandkids or me again. You won't be able to come to our wedding, nothing." I know it's playing dirty, and I hate to do it, especially with her in the hospital like this. But I can't live in fear anymore. I have to know she is going to do the right thing and put that bastard behind bars.

After a few minutes of silence, Mom nods her head slightly. "Okay, I'll press charges," she says in a soft voice.

When I sigh in relief, Dean squeezes my hand reassuringly.

The next few days fly by in a blur. Mom stays in the hospital, and Dean and his friends take turns standing guard outside her room. I visit her as much as possible, checking in on her and attempting to keep her spirits up.

Today, I am joined by Courtney and Jensen, who will be helping her get back on her feet. The place my mom rents with my stepdad is in his name, and with him in jail, the landlord wants them out. Not that my mom can afford the place on her own, anyway.

So, when my mom is released tomorrow, a bunch of the Riders are going to town, to help pack up everything and put it in storage. Then Mom is going to go stay at the women's shelter for a week until Dean and I get settled in his cabin. Then she will be with us for the holidays, and Courtney and Jensen will help her get a job and a place of her own.

Everything is finally starting to come together.

CHAPTER 12
DEAN

THANKFULLY, once Holly's mom agreed to press charges, things moved pretty quickly. Law enforcement was dead set on not letting him get away because he was one of the first higher ranking guys they had been able to bust in the Savage Bones.

While her stepdad isn't in leadership, he's a patched member and much more valuable than the other thugs they've caught. Until now, Savage Bones has been pretty good at evading law enforcement.

The Mustang Mountain Riders know that we now have a target on our back with the Savage Bones, but we probably had one, anyway. The feeling is that they are planning on moving in on our town.

After they ran her stepdad's fingerprints, they were able to also attach him to several more crimes, and it looks like he's going to be spending over ten years in jail.

Holly's mom has been brave in taking the steps to dig out and become independent. While staying at the women's shelter, she enjoyed reading to the kids and playing with them. Also, she had fun spending time in the nursery helping with the babies that the women's shelter watches over while the women there are doing interviews, working, and getting their new places all set up.

Just yesterday, the woman who has been in charge of the daycare and nursery at the shelter announced that she was leaving. She's going back home to Maine to help take care of her mother.

Courtney didn't even hesitate. She offered the job to Holly's mom, who accepted on the spot. After everything that they have done to help her, she's excited to be able to continue to help at the women's shelter.

True to our word, The Mustang Mountain Riders have helped her every step of the way. From clearing out the apartment and getting everything into storage, to getting her set up in her new place and even helping her file for divorce. If there is a trial for what he did to her, we will be there by her side.

With her mom doing so well, Holly and I decided that we want to get married as soon as possible. As in, before the first of the year. We want to start the new year as husband and wife. So, we will have a New Year's Eve wedding, allowing all the Riders to be together for the event and, of course, a great New Year's party.

The other women have taken her under their wing and have been helping with all the wedding planning.

As far as I know, we have been staying under the radar with Ruby until today.

I'm heading to the mercantile to let her know and see if she can pull a few strings with her husband to get the wedding moving along.

Walking into the mercantile, I see Ruby standing behind the register. The little bell above the door chimes, alerting her to my presence.

"Hey there, Dean. What can I do for you?"

I take a deep breath before speaking. "I need to talk to you about something important."

Ruby's face pulls into a concerned expression. "What's going on? Are you okay?"

"I'm fine. I just thought I'd invite you and Orville to my wedding on New Year's Eve," I say with a smile.

Ruby's eyes go wide as saucers. One hand goes over her heart, and the other has a death grip on the counter.

"Wedding? To whom? How did you meet? How did I not know? I knew I was getting older, but I didn't think my senses would go all at once! Sit down and tell me everything!"

"Don't worry, you aren't slipping from your gossip queen status. Her name is Holly. I was helping her find a safe place for her and her kids. She was staying at the shelter. We have been hiding away at my parents' cabin, so there was no way for anyone to know."

"Oh, my heavens. You mountain men sure do move fast once you fall in love... wait, did you say she had kids?"

"Yes, Max, who is six, and Gracie, who is four."

"Oh, I am so happy for you! What can I do to help?" She pulls out a notepad and pencil.

"Well, if he's willing, we'd love for Orville to marry us."

"We'd be offended if you asked anyone else! Where are you getting married?"

"At the clubhouse. Holly's only family is her mom. Other than my mom and dad, the rest of my family are the Riders. You and Orville will be our guests of honor." Then I go on to explain that we have a strict rule about nonmembers of the club not being allowed inside the clubhouse.

"It's been years since I've been there. I'd love to see what you guys have done with it. What about Holly? Does she have a dress, flowers, cake? Oh, and I need to meet her!"

Just then, the door chimes, and in walks my beautiful bride-to-be.

"Sorry, I'm late!" Holly says. She had texted me about the traffic leaving Whitefish, and I said I would

103

talk to Ruby and meet her at home, but I'm glad she decided to join me.

"Well, you can meet her now. Holly, this is Ruby, the Mayor's wife. Ruby, this is Holly, my fiancé."

"Well, aren't you just the prettiest thing this side of the Mississippi!" Ruby rushes to give her a hug.

"Ruby, to answer your questions. She just got her dress today. Everly's mom is going to tailor it for her. Lily is making the cake and food, and Jenna and Emma are taking care of the flowers," I say.

"We just need some help with decorations and set up the day of," Holly says.

"Well, you let me handle all that. What colors have you chosen? What style? We have so many decorations from the city events we can dig into," Ruby says.

"Is it corny to go with white, gold, silver, and bronze for a New Year's Eve wedding?" Holly asks.

"No, I love it! We have the perfect decorations for it, too!" Ruby says.

"Also, I really want to include lace. I always thought lace was so fancy, and I wanted it for my wedding," Holly adds.

"Done! Oh, I am so excited! What better way to end the year in Mustang Mountain than with a wedding!"

"I think being able to call you my wife is the perfect way to end the year." I pull Holly into my arms.

"I couldn't agree more." She beams a bright smile back at me.

I hate to admit that Ruby can add another win to her books, but I wouldn't change a single thing. It brought me my family.

EPILOGUE

EVEN THOUGH I didn't believe love between a man and a woman could last forever, it had been a beautiful wedding. I'd stood next to my brother while he vowed to love, honor, cherish, and protect his new bride until death do they part. I was glad Dean had found someone to share his life with, even if I thought he was a sap.

It had been a rough couple of weeks in Mustang Mountain, and as I made my way home, all I wanted was to fall into bed and sleep for the next few days. I'd expected to see a few other cars on the road, probably stragglers heading home from New Year's Eve parties, but snow blanketed the empty streets.

After all of the excitement around town, I welcomed the peace and quiet. With luck, the new year would bring more of both. We sure could use a break. My fellow Mustang Mountain Riders and I had been working around the clock to figure out why a one-percent MC was trying to edge in on our turf. With the main threat behind bars, I hoped we'd put a stop to whatever plans they might have to take over Mustang Mountain. All in all, things were looking up, and I was ready for it.

I turned off the radio and welcomed the comforting silence. The DJ had blasted top forty hits all night long and my ears were still ringing from the assault. As I glanced up, a dark figure flew out of the woods and crossed right in front of my truck. I slammed on the brakes but felt the impact as I clipped the animal on the front passenger side.

Fuck. I'd just had a dent repaired from the last dumbass deer who'd tried to tangle with my half-ton pickup. I pulled over to the side of the narrow mountain road and grabbed the flashlight I always carried with me as well as the revolver from my center console. If the animal was severely injured, the right thing to do would be to put it out of its misery.

Rounding the front of the truck, I glanced down, expecting to see the twisted body of a deer. My pulse spiked at the sight captured in the wide beam of the flashlight. Her red hair stood out in stark contrast to the snow underneath her. What the fuck was a woman doing out in the woods at this time of night?

I crouched down and rested my fingers on her neck, checking her vitals. She was breathing, thank fuck. The impact from the truck must have knocked her out cold. I needed to get her to a hospital, and fast. I pulled my phone out of my back pocket to call 911.

Service was spotty on the drive up the mountain, and it was just my luck that my truck sat in one of the dead zones. I couldn't leave her there on the side of the road, but I didn't want to risk moving her unless I could assess her injuries and make sure I wouldn't make things worse.

I moved the flashlight over her still form. She had on ripped jeans and a pair of high-top sneakers. Blood covered her chest. Grabbing the stupid pocket square that came with the tux I'd rented for the wedding, I moved closer to see if I could figure out where it was coming from. My hand shook as I touched the handkerchief to her skin.

The blood wasn't from an injury, it was from a tattoo. A recent tattoo based on the color of her skin underneath the thick, dark lines. As I gently sopped up the blood, the design became clearer. It was a snake with a pair of dice where its eyes should have been. I didn't have a clue about what it could mean until I saw the logo the serpent's tail coiled around—a skull with the words Savage Bones marked across the bottom.

I dropped the handkerchief and stood, bracing myself for whatever might come charging out of the woods. The silence was deafening. On a clear night like this, I'd be able to hear the snap of a twig echo in the darkness for half a mile, yet I heard nothing.

Either no one was following her or they were biding their time.

The woman moaned. I wouldn't leave her, even if she did belong to the MC who'd been threatening the safety of Mustang Mountain. And taking her to the hospital was out of the question. Based on what she was wearing, she looked like she'd left in a hurry. If she'd been running from a member of the Savage Bones, they'd be scouring the hospitals in the area, hoping she'd turn up.

Until I knew why she'd been running down the mountain in the middle of the night, I'd have to take her somewhere safe. I bent down and being as gentle as I could, I scooped her into my arms. She winced, but nestled into my chest as I cradled her against me. Her skin was like ice, freezing cold to the touch. I needed to get her warmed up and cleaned up as quickly as possible so I could get a better idea of the extent of her injuries.

If my phone had service, I'd be able to call one of my Mustang Mountain Riders brothers. Dean deserved the night off, but any one of them would drop everything and head my way at a moment's notice.

I held her in my arms and pulled open the door to the backseat. It wouldn't be the smoothest ride, but I'd go as slow as I could. With her secured in the backseat and a spare blanket tucked around her, I got behind the wheel and turned around on the narrow road. Without knowing where she'd come from, I didn't want to head back up the mountain.

There was only one place to take her where she would be safe. I headed toward the edge of town, hellbent on getting to the clubhouse before whoever might be looking for her found us.

WANT MORE DEAN AND HOLLY? **Sign up for our newsletter** and get the free bonus scene here: https://www.matchofthemonthbooks.com/Dean-Bonus

GET Six's and Bear's stories in The Mustang Mountain Riders. Start with January's Ride with Six (https://www.matchofthemonthbooks.com/January-Six) and February's Ride With Bear (https://www.matchofthemonthbooks.com/February-Bear)

MOUNTAIN MEN OF MUSTANG MOUNTAIN

Welcome to Mustang Mountain where love runs as wild as the free-spirited horses who roam the hillsides. Framed by rivers, lakes, and breathtaking mountains, it's also the place the Mountain Men of Mustang Mountain call home. They might be rugged and reclusive, but they'll risk their hearts for the curvy girls they love.

To learn more about the Mountain Men of Mustang Mountain, visit our website (https://www.matchofthemonthbooks.com/) join our newsletter here (http://subscribepage.io/MatchOfTheMonth) or follow our Patreon for extra bonus content here (https://www.patreon.com/MatchOfTheMonth)

January is for Jackson - https://www.matchofthemonthbooks.com/January-Jackson

February is for Ford - https://www.matchofthemonthbooks.com/February-Ford

March is for Miles - https://www.matchofthemonthbooks.com/March-Miles

April is for Asher -
https://www.matchofthemonthbooks.com/April-Asher
May is for Mack -
https://www.matchofthemonthbooks.com/May-Mack
June is for Jensen -
https://www.matchofthemonthbooks.com/June-Jensen
July is for Jonas -
https://www.matchofthemonthbooks.com/July-Jonas
August is for Ace -
https://www.matchofthemonthbooks.com/AceAugust
September is for Shaw -
https://www.matchofthemonthbooks.com/September-Shaw
October is for Owen -
https://www.matchofthemonthbooks.com/October-Owen
November is for Nate -
https://www.matchofthemonthbooks.com/November-Nate
December is for Dean -
https://www.matchofthemonthbooks.com/December-Dean

ACKNOWLEDGMENTS

A huge, heartfelt thanks goes to everyone who's supported us in our writing, especially our HUSSIES of Mountain Men of Mustang Mountain patrons:

Jackie Ziegler

To learn more about the Mountain Men of Mustang Mountain on Patreon, visit us here: https://www.patreon.com/MatchOfTheMonth

OTHER BOOKS BY KACI ROSE

Oakside Military Heroes Series

Saving Noah – Lexi and Noah

Saving Easton – Easton and Paisley

Saving Teddy – Teddy and Mia

Saving Levi – Levi and Mandy

Saving Gavin – Gavin and Lauren

Saving Logan – Logan and Faith

Saving Ethan – Bri and Ethan

Saving Zane — Zane

Mountain Men of Whiskey River

Take Me To The River – Axel and Emelie

Take Me To The Cabin – Phoenix and Jenna

Take Me To The Lake – Cash and Hope

Taken by The Mountain Man - Cole and Jana

Take Me To The Mountain – Bennett and Willow

Take Me To The Edge – Storm and River

Mountain Men of Mustang Mountain

February is for Ford – Ford and Luna

April is for Asher – Asher and Jenna

June is for Jensen - Jensen and Courtney

August is for Ace - Ace and Everly

Club Red – Short Stories

Daddy's Dare – Knox and Summer

Sold to my Ex's Dad - Evan and Jana

Jingling His Bells – Zion and Emma

Club Red: Chicago

Elusive Dom

Forbidden Dom

Chasing the Sun Duet

Sunrise – Kade and Lin

Sunset – Jasper and Brynn

Rock Stars of Nashville

She's Still The One – Dallas and Austin

Standalone Books

Texting Titan - Denver and Avery

Accidental Sugar Daddy – Owen and Ellie

Stay With Me Now – David and Ivy

Midnight Rose - Ruby and Orlando

Committed Cowboy – Whiskey Run Cowboys

Stalking His Obsession - Dakota and Grant

Falling in Love on Route 66 - Weston and Rory

Billionaire's Marigold - Mari and Dalton

A Baby for Her Best Friend – Nick and Summer

CONNECT WITH KACI ROSE

Website
Facebook
Kaci Rose Reader's Facebook Group
TikTok
Instagram
Twitter
Goodreads
Book Bub
Join Kaci Rose's VIP List (Newsletter)

ABOUT KACI ROSE

Kaci Rose writes steamy contemporary romance mostly set in small towns. She grew up in Florida but longs for the mountains over the beach.

She is a mom to 5 kids, a dog who is scared of his own shadow, and a puppy who's actively destroying her house.

She also writes steamy cowboy romance as Kaci M. Rose.

PLEASE LEAVE A REVIEW!

I love to hear from my readers! Please **head over to your favorite store and leave a review** of what you thought of this book!

Made in the USA
Columbia, SC
23 September 2024

42131087R00075